RUNNING FROM THE PAST

Katie Reus

Running From the Past/Katie Reus. -- 1st ed.

ISBN-13: 978-1502486134
ISBN-10: 150248613X

eBook ISBN: 9780996087469

For my husband. Thank you for your endless support.

Praise for the novels of Katie Reus

"Sinful, Sexy, Suspense... Katie Reus pulls you in and never lets go."
—*New York Times* bestselling author, Laura Wright

"Has all the right ingredients: a hot couple, evil villains, and a killer action-filled plot. . . . [The] Moon Shifter series is what I call Grade-A entertainment!" —Joyfully Reviewed

"Reus strikes just the right balance of steamy sexual tension and nail-biting action....This romantic thriller reliably hits every note that fans of the genre will expect." —*Publisher's Weekly*

"Explosive danger and enough sexual tension to set the pages on fire . . . fabulous!" —*New York Times* bestselling author, Alexandra Ivy

"Nonstop action, a solid plot, good pacing and riveting suspense..."
—*RT Book Reviews (4.5 Stars)*

"Wow! This powerful, passionate hero sizzles with sheer deliciousness. I loved every sexy twist of this fun & exhilarating tale. Katie Reus delivers!" —Carolyn Crane, RITA award winning author

Continued...

"You'll fall in love with Katie's heroes." —*New York Times* bestselling author, Kaylea Cross

"A sexy, well-crafted paranormal romance that succeeds with smart characters and creative world building."—Kirkus Reviews

"*Mating Instinct*'s romance is taut and passionate . . . Katie Reus's newest installment in her Moon Shifter series will leave readers breathless!" —Stephanie Tyler, *New York Times* bestselling author

"Reus has definitely hit a home run with this series. . . . This book has mystery, suspense, and a heart-pounding romance that will leave you wanting more." —Nocturne Romance Reads

"Katie Reus pulls the reader into a story line of second chances, betrayal, and the truth about forgotten lives and hidden pasts." —The Reading Café

"If you are looking for a really good, new military romance series, pick up *Targeted*! The new Deadly Ops series stands to be a passionate and action-riddled read." —That's What I'm Talking About

"I could not put this book down. . . . Let me be clear that I am not saying that this was a good book *for* a paranormal genre; it was an excellent romance read, *period*." —All About Romance

CHAPTER ONE

Emma Garcia gripped the steering wheel of the stolen pickup truck she wished she wasn't driving. In the entirety of her twenty six years, she hadn't taken as much as a piece of gum without paying for it. Until today.

Today.

Oh how she wished she could go back and pretend today hadn't happened. Just go about her daily life and pretend . . . no, she couldn't. Not if she wanted to be able to look at herself in the mirror every morning. Why even pretend she could? She'd already had to pull over twice to puke.

After four and half hours on the road she hadn't dared go over the speed limit by more than two miles. She couldn't afford to get pulled over for something so stupid. Not when she'd come so far.

Her cell phone rang and she jumped, swerving slightly into the left lane. A soccer mom driving an SUV gave her the finger. Classy.

The harsh blare of the phone invaded the quiet cabin of the dingy truck. She hadn't even realized that the radio was off until now. One look at the name displayed on the screen and bile involuntarily rose in her throat. Ricardo.

Before she could change her mind she slid her finger across the screen to answer, reminding herself to act natural. "Hello." To her own ears she sounded calm, although she couldn't imagine how. Not when her heart beat an erratic tattoo against her ribcage and she gripped the steering wheel so tightly she'd left claw marks in the vinyl.

"Where are you?" he demanded. Always with the demands because he couldn't ever just talk to her like a normal person.

She gritted her teeth despite the fear bubbling up inside of her at just hearing his icy voice. "Out shopping." That was a safe lie.

"When will you be home?"

She scanned the rearview mirror in a blind panic. It wasn't likely he knew she'd left Miami, but her paranoia ran bone deep. After what she'd witnessed, she had a reason to be wary. "In a couple hours. I'm getting a pedicure and manicure later."

He was silent, which wasn't unusual, but today that could mean anything. Finally he spoke and she wasn't prepared for the question. "Why is your car still here?"

She inwardly cringed. Shit, shit, *shit*! Her brand new SLR McLaren Roadster still sat in the four car garage so she blurted the first thing that popped into her mind. "Amber picked me up. We're having a girl's day."

"Hmm. Amber called the house not ten minutes ago looking for you. She said she tried your cell phone but couldn't get through."

Emma swallowed hard. Phone service on I-75 was sporadic at best. She turned on her blinker and took the next exit. She couldn't drive and have this conversation at the same time. Better to go on the offensive. "Why do you even care where I am? I don't ask you questions about your social life or extracurricular activities." She didn't bother to hide the sarcasm in her voice.

He snorted and she could just picture him standing with his hands on his hips, overlooking the Atlantic Ocean from the three story balcony of his palatial Mediterranean style home. Thinking he was God. "I don't give a shit what you're doing or who you're doing it with. I just don't want you lying to me. We have a deal."

"Correction. We *had* a deal. Now that my mom is dead, you have nothing to hold over me."

He sighed and though miles separated them, she could visualize his cold blue eyes boring into her, daring her to defy him. He'd no doubt change tactics and try to appease her. Like always. Only this time it wouldn't work. "Come on Emma, there's a dinner tonight at the—"

"I don't care what dinner you have planned or how important it is, I'm not going. We're through. Do you understand?" Her voice shook. The only reason she felt safe talking to him this was because she didn't plan on seeing him again.

There was a long pause in which she wondered where that burst of defiance had come from. "I thought you were happy with our arrangement. I buy you whatever you want and all I ask in return is that you accompany me to public outings. I even support that stupid homeless shelter you volunteer at." His voice was filled with derision.

She ground her teeth so hard she was surprised she didn't chip a tooth. If he'd thought her happy, then he was more delusional than she thought. "You threatened my mother if I didn't agree to your demands! I just want a normal life, why can't you find someone else for your pathetic charade?"

He let out a low chuckle, completely without mirth. "Maybe you're not hearing me. You *belong* to me. I was going to announce tonight that we will marry in a year. The time has come. If I don't propose soon, people will begin to wonder why I give you so much freedom."

She steered the truck into a crowded Publix parking lot, and ignored the safe feeling she got when surrounded by people, even though two days ago she wouldn't have thought twice about sitting alone in a parked car. Now she knew better.

Something about his condescending tone rattled and for the first time in years, actually annoyed her. Maybe it was the horror she'd witnessed that morning, or maybe it was eight years of dealing with his chauvinistic, pompous, 'the world owes me something' attitude. She'd heard the rumors, but hadn't truly believed them until now. There was no hiding the disgust in her voice. "If you think I'm going to voluntarily marry you, you're out of your freaking mind. Just leave me alone and I won't tell anyone your secret."

The *secret* she referred to wasn't his profession. He barely tried to hide that. No, this was something he kept from the world.

He ignored her outburst and promise of silence, as if she hadn't spoken at all. "Your mother died months ago. Why are you doing this now? I haven't even seen you in a month..." Ricardo abruptly stopped and her stomach roiled violently.

She began to tremble. *He knew.* She didn't know how, but he did.

Neither spoke for several moments until finally he broke into her thoughts. "Tell me what you saw Emma."

The phone slipped in her sweaty palm, but she managed to keep it against her ear. "Nothing." The word came out a whisper.

She heard him rummaging with something in the background. "Is that why half your clothes and all your jewelry are gone?"

Emma closed her eyes, massaged her temple with her free hand, and ended the call. Her next move was to turn it completely off and take out the battery. Ricardo had a long arm, and she knew people could be tracked using the GPS in cell phones. That was the same reason she hadn't taken the new Mercedes he'd bought her as an early Christmas gift. That would have been like putting out a homing beacon for him.

She glanced in the rearview mirror and blanched at her reflection. She had no makeup on, and the dark half-moons under her eyes gave her a haunted look. As she brushed a strand of her long blond hair back, an idea struck her. She didn't know where she was going, but she knew she needed to change her appearance. And fast.

Ricardo had insisted she keep her hair platinum blond so that would be the first thing to go. She was a natural brunette so changing it would be easy enough. She had close to one thousand dollars in her purse, not including all her jewelry which was worth at least thirty times that, but the money wouldn't last her long and she couldn't risk pawning the jewelry just yet. That was for emergencies only.

"Okay, all I need to do is reinvent myself, find a place to hide, and get a job. Should be easy enough." She said the words aloud in a pathetic attempt to convince herself.

Nothing about this was going to be easy. Not when she had no clue where she was headed, or what to do with the information in her head. She couldn't go to the police in Miami. Even if they put her in protective custody, she wouldn't last two days, probably even less. On that, she'd stake her life. The only person she could trust right now, was herself.

CHAPTER TWO

Caleb Ryder took off his Stetson and wiped the sweat and grime from his brow. He breathed in the crisp country air, when a deep, rumbling sound interrupted his walk from the horse stables to his house. Lifting his hand to block the sun, he looked to the west to see a dusty, beat-up truck inching down the driveway, shooting out white smoke and kicking up dirt every few feet.

He glanced at his watch out of habit, even though he knew it was a little after five. If this was another traveling salesman, he didn't have the time. Normally he didn't quit work until at least six, sometimes seven but since Rachel, his full time housekeeper, had up and gotten married on him, he had no one to prepare meals for his men. Almost four weeks had passed and not one single person had answered his ad, so he'd been stuck cooking.

The truck careened through the main gate, sputtered once more and jerked to a halt. Before he could prepare a mental "get lost" speech, a petite, dark-haired woman with impossibly full lips stepped out of the truck. For a moment, he forgot to breathe. She was his walking, breathing, living fantasy. She pushed her sunglasses back to reveal dark, stunning eyes. Eyes a man could lose himself forever in. *Shit*, where had that thought come from?

Despite her simple clothes, everything about her was graceful, stunning even. Her long, brown hair was pulled back in a ponytail and though she wore a clingy turtleneck and jeans, he'd bet anything her outfit, including the sunglasses, cost more than the truck she drove.

Expensive. It was the one word he could think of to describe her. Hell, close up, she even smelled expensive. Something indefinable and erotic teased his nose. Flowery, but not overwhelming. Just enough to make him want more. She must be lost. It was the only explanation.

"Hello, I'm Emma G-Cole." She coughed and half-smiled as she held out a delicate hand.

It took him a moment to comprehend what she wanted. "Um, yeah, hello," he grunted and grabbed her small hand in his, then wanted to kick himself. He was nasty, dirty and he smelled like a horse. Literally.

She faltered a bit but was polite enough not to wipe off her hand. "I'm here about the job."

When he didn't respond, she continued and he didn't miss the uncertainty in her voice. "For the cook?"

Was this some kind of joke? She wanted to cook for him and fifteen of his men? Cowhands and horse trainers? Why would a woman who could easily be a face model want to work in Lake City, Florida, the middle of nowhere? Okay, maybe nowhere was a bit of a stretch but with a population of a little more than ten thousand, it wasn't an overly active city and he wasn't even in the city limits.

She shifted her feet and her toothpaste-commercial smile fell. Shit, he still hadn't given her an answer and he'd been staring a lot harder than was socially acceptable. He cleared his throat but didn't break her gaze. "Yes ma'am, the position's still open. I should warn you that it doesn't pay much but room and board are covered. You'd be in charge of cooking breakfast and dinner for at least fifteen men, five days a week. On weekends, they fend for themselves. You'd also be responsible for cleaning the main house." He paused and let his eyes trail to her hands. Fine-boned, slim hands that looked like they hadn't seen a day of hard labor.

She must have noticed his appraisal because she clasped her hands together and clenched them so tightly her olive skin turned white.

"I come from a big Cuban family so I'm used to cooking for large numbers and I have no problem cleaning. As long as you're not an unusual pig, I don't foresee any difficulty," she said in a tone that suggested she was used to bossing people around.

As long as he wasn't a pig? Oh yeah, she was definitely a princess. And a bossy one at that.

He let out a bark of laughter. Normally he'd do a more extensive interview but what choice did he have? It wasn't as if people were lining up for the position and he was afraid his men would mutiny if they had to suffer through another night of his cooking. "All right, I'll have to do a background check, show you the kitchen to see if you think you can handle it, then—"

"No." She crossed her arms over her chest and set her jaw.

"Uh, no what? You don't want to see the kitchen?"

"No background checks. I'm not giving you my social security number."

He stood there quietly, watching her, trying to figure out what was going on in that pretty head. Desperation and defiance were an odd mix but the emotions played across her upturned face in equal measures. Caleb knew he should just tell her to turn around and leave but something in her deep brown eyes called to his protective nature. Something primitive and unfamiliar inside him stirred. "Why?"

She swallowed but instead of turning and running as expected, she answered. "I just broke off an engagement with someone and my family is less than thrilled with me. I need space and I need to make it on my own without my family butting in."

After twelve years as a Marine Corps scout sniper, he was better than most at reading people's faces. If there was one thing he knew, it was if someone wasn't being straight with him. Her story was good and she obviously thought quickly on her feet but it was a lie. He'd let it slide. For now. "Then why can't I do a background check?"

"If you run my number, my family will find me."

"How?"

Her face paled and something flared in her eyes. Something he'd seen on the battlefield more times than he could count. Fear. Real, unabashed, almost tangible terror. "They just would. Trust me," she muttered and shifted her feet again.

He didn't respond, forcing her to break the silence. "I know you haven't had any responses to your ad..."

"How the fu— how do you know that?" he demanded.

A pinkish tinge of color ran across her high, exotic cheekbones. "Alice Delaney told me you were looking for someone and she also said you were the worst cook south of the Mason-Dixon line. So I know you need someone badly and I need a job. Maybe we can strike a deal. I cook for a week and if you're not satisfied, I leave. You don't even have to pay me."

Her mouth snapped shut and those damn expressive eyes widened expectantly, luring him in. Oh she was trouble all right. No doubt about it.

Caleb was going to tell her to leave. It was on the tip of his tongue. How could he hire someone without any references? And Alice, the owner of Delaney's Bed and Breakfast, didn't exactly count. She was close to a hundred and trusted everyone.

All his experience told him this would pan out badly—because this woman was trouble—but he wasn't thinking with his head. No, he was thinking with a much lower part of his anatomy. The part that wondered what was underneath that formfitting sweater. Her breasts were small, just like the rest of her but he'd bet anything she had perfect, pink nipples. Perfect for sucking and kissing. "When can you start?"

Confusion flitted across her features, as if she'd expected him to tell her to leave but it was quickly replaced by a blinding, megawatt smile. "Tonight if you want. If you haven't already started dinner, I can do it."

"Don't you need to go back and get your stuff from Alice's?"

She shook her head. "No. Everything I own is in the truck. If you weren't hiring, I was going to keep moving north."

The thought of her driving along the highway at night, by herself, caused that stupid protective urge to jump in his gut again. "Where are your bags?"

"In the back but I can get..."

He didn't let her finish. He opened the back door and pulled out two large Louis Vuitton bags and he very much doubted they were fakes.

"I said I can—"

Ignoring the sweet scent teasing his nose and her protestations, he shut the door and turned to face her. "Do you know where you're going?"

"Well, no," she faltered.

"I do." He turned on his heel and led her up to the main house.

He stalked down the gravel driveway, through the two-car garage attached to the kitchen, slung open the side door and waited for her to enter. As she passed, she glanced at him and for the first time he saw a trace of unease. Good. The more he thought about her situation, or what she'd said of it, the more pissed he got. She'd practically announced that no one except Alice knew she was at the ranch. For all she knew, he could be dangerous.

Which he was. But not to her. Never to her.

But she didn't know that. What if she'd trusted the wrong person and not him? The thought caused a strange squeezing sensation in his lungs. That stupid protective urge was back.

"You have a lovely house." Her soft voice startled him out of his contemplations.

"Thank you, my father built it." He led her down the long hallway to her new living quarters.

His father had built the country style house for his mother forty years ago. Five years before he'd been born and ten before his mother had died. The back side of the house was almost all windows, overlooking a small creek and hundreds of acres of rolling, lush land. The living room and family room had spectacular views perfect for entertaining, which had been his father's original intention.

They passed the door to the master bedroom on the way to the stairs when a sudden image of Emma flat on her back, naked, long hair pillowed out, framing her face and body, appeared. It had been at least a year since he'd had sex or any interest in sex but now his dick decided to wake up. Fucking great.

The thought of having to share the same roof and know he couldn't touch her was going to drive him slowly mad. Starting something with an employee was something he'd ever done, nor planned to do now. He shouldn't have hired her. It was probably the dumbest thing he'd ever done in fact. Including the rose tattoo he had on his ass after losing a bet when he'd been in the Marines. He inwardly sighed and led her up the stairs.

One week. He'd promised her that. After it was over, he'd send her on her way.

"This is it. You have a sundeck through the French doors. It's not big but it'll give you privacy. The other two bedrooms across the hall share a bathroom but you have a private one. Again, it's not big—"

"Everything's fine, really."

He nodded, put the bags down at the end of the queen-sized bed and when he turned around, noticed the light circles under her eyes. His gut twisted. She looked ready to pass out on her feet.

Before he had a chance to think about her condition, she tossed her purse on the bed, put her hands on her slim hips and smiled. "Let's get to that kitchen."

CHAPTER THREE

Emma surveyed the open, colorful kitchen after Caleb left. It had been decorated in a traditional country theme with rooster accessories, bright daffodil and cherry colored walls and vintage framed sepia prints depicting farm life. The style wasn't something she'd have chosen but it fit with the old-fashioned theme of the rest of the house.

When she opened the oversized, stainless steel fridge, she grimaced. Meat and more meat. He obviously hadn't been shopping for foodstuff in a while. At least she had enough for the evening and for breakfast. She could go shopping tomorrow and hit up the local library in the process. More than groceries, she needed Internet access and privacy.

Shaking her head, she pulled out two bags of yellow rice and a few cans of black beans. It was hard to believe Caleb hired her, especially since she'd behaved like a lunatic criminal. He'd almost told her to get lost. The look in his eyes had been unmistakable.

But he hadn't. Maybe he really was desperate. Which was damn good for her.

What she was doing was stupid, she knew that but she needed to put her feet down and think about her next move. She couldn't keep traveling north with no real plan and limited funds. Though she'd only been gone two days, she had no doubt Ricardo had already sent people after her. Dangerous people. People who wouldn't think twice about hurting anyone within a hundred mile radius if it meant silencing her forever.

She was scared but not as much as she should be. All she could seem to focus on was the very sexy man who'd hired her. The small, jagged, almost invisible scar along his left cheek gave Caleb a primitive, dark look. Like a warrior. A shiver ran down her spine when an image of his lips pressed against hers flashed in her mind. Her libido had been in hibernation for so many years it was embarrassing. Now was *not* the time for it to spring to life.

In her gut, she knew Caleb was a dangerous man but she also knew he wasn't dangerous to her. When he'd insisted on carrying her bags, she'd simply known what kind of man he was. She was the hired help and he still treated her with respect.

For eight years, she'd been Ricardo's supposed woman and not once had he ever done anything remotely like that. All she'd been was a piece of arm candy. "Look pretty and smile for the camera", he'd told her more than once. And he'd usually been digging his brutal fingers into her arm when he said it. He'd always been such a bastard even when there was no reason to be. But cruelty didn't have to make sense.

Caleb was a far cry from Ricardo in looks. Ricardo had the pretty boy appearance down to an art. He was the typical rich playboy—dark hair, perfect olive skin, always well groomed, going so far as to get his eyebrows waxed bi-weekly. And that was usually followed by a manicure. Pathetic really. He was higher maintenance than any woman she knew.

There was nothing pretty about Caleb. No sir. He was all man, probably weighing in at around two hundred pounds of pure steel. His faded button-down flannel shirt had been rolled up at the sleeves to reveal tight, corded muscles, tanned skin and a couple of tattoos. Not exceptionally tall, maybe five feet eleven inches, but he still towered over her five feet two inches. Not so much with his height but his presence altogether. She couldn't help but wonder if that dominating authority extended to the bedroom.

As her treacherous mind fantasized about her new employer, she forced herself to focus on the task at hand. She pulled out a pot, filled it with water, a bit of olive oil and began her preparations. Cooking for sixteen was no different than cooking for two. Just add more ingredients. She wasn't sure how anyone could be as terrible at cooking as Alice described but the white-haired woman didn't give the impression of one who exaggerated often. Once the rice was simmering and the chicken baking, she rummaged through his pantry trying to find stuff for breakfast when her hand strayed across a large package of sponge cakes. Not exactly lady fingers but she'd make do if he had the rest of the basic ingredients for tiramisu. Her tiramisu was to die for and it just might convince him to keep her.

She turned the radio on low and let herself relax. Well, as much as she could under the circumstances. Growing up, the kitchen had been her haven but in recent years the only times she'd ever cooked for pleasure had been at her mother's house during the holidays. Other than that, Ricardo's chef had always been on hand, or she'd eaten out with friends.

Half an hour later, men trickled through the kitchen in groups of two and three. Each one gave her a surprised look but took off their hats and mumbled a polite greeting. She grinned to herself. Maybe it wasn't just Caleb, maybe grunting was how cowboys communicated.

The kitchen was attached to an informal dining room the men wandered into. Luckily a wall separated her from their curious eyes. Today of all days she didn't need extra scrutiny. Despite changing her platinum blonde hair back to her natural chestnut, her paranoia ran bone deep. If she wanted to keep this job, she needed to be invisible. Even though she managed to grab all her jewelry during her escape, selling it was for emergencies only. The measly thousand dollars in her purse wouldn't last long and she couldn't afford to use her credit card.

She glanced at the rooster wall clock, then peeked around the corner. Fifteen in all but Caleb was nowhere to be seen. One of the younger men noticed her and smiled, causing fourteen other pairs of eyes to turn in her direction. Emma stepped under the archway, tried to ignore the feeling of being on display and addressed the man closest to her. "I'm not sure how you gentleman normally do this but the food's ready so should I just bring it in and place it on the table?"

At once, four men stood and shook their heads. The one she addressed, a young man with sandy blond hair probably no older than eighteen or nineteen also stood and smiled sheepishly, his face lighting up like Rudolph's nose. "No ma'am, we'll carry everything in."

Since she'd already placed a large bowl of Caesar salad on each end of the long, wooden rectangular table, they carried the two serving dishes of baked chicken and three bowls of rice and beans out for her. Still no sign of Caleb.

"Should someone maybe tell Caleb that dinner is ready?"

Before anyone could answer, a deep voice from behind startled her. "No need."

Still standing under the large archway, she pivoted on her heels and sucked in a breath. Gone was the rough looking cowboy. Clean shaven and free of dirt, Caleb looked good enough to eat. A navy blue polo t-shirt stretched across his broad, muscular chest and his dark jeans showcased equally muscular legs. That primitive look in his piercing green eyes wasn't gone and something told her it might never go away.

She half motioned with her hand to the dining room where the men had already started scooping large portions of everything onto their plates. "Everything's on the table. You might want to get some before it's gone."

"Aren't you going to join us?" He still hadn't made a move to join the men.

She shook her head and ignored the foreign feminine flutter in her stomach. "No, I'm still working on dessert and I'm getting a couple of quiches ready for tomorrow."

"Quiche?" The blank look on his rugged face made her smile. His dark brow furrowed together and for a moment, she glimpsed a softer side of him.

"Trust me, your men will like it and so will you." She smothered a grin and hurried past him back into the bright kitchen, ignoring the jolt of awareness that surged through her when her hip brushed his. She really didn't need to work on dessert. The tiramisu was in the refrigerator and putting the sausage and cheese quiche together was simple. She'd be done before they finished eating but she didn't want to risk having to answer any personal questions or being recognized. She hadn't exactly worked out a cover story yet and was too tired to think on her feet.

And if she was really honest, she didn't want to dine with Caleb. Just standing near him did funny things to her stomach. Enduring an entire meal was too much for her fuzzy brain.

Appreciative grunts and not much conversation greeted her ears, so she pulled out a cookbook and browsed through it. If they were satisfied with a meal that simple, they were in for a surprise. About thirty minutes later, a man in his late forties whom she guessed to be Native American, walked in carrying an empty plate. "What would you like me to do with this ma'am?"

She held out a hand and took the plate with a smile. "I'll take care of this and you don't have to call me ma'am. Emma is fine."

Before he could protest and she knew he was about to because he had the same look in his eyes Caleb had when he'd insisted on carrying her bags, she continued. "Did they send you in here?"

His face slightly reddened and he nodded. "We used to leave our plates for Rachel but none of the guys wanted to insult you."

She smiled again. They were all so polite. It was a nice change of pace from the people she was used to. "Is everyone else about through?"

He nodded. "Yes ma'am."

She smothered a sigh. Maybe calling her ma'am was a southern thing. She'd grown up in Miami and while it was technically one of the southernmost parts of the United States, it wasn't exactly the Deep South.

"Okay, well if you'll help me gather up the rest of the plates, I'll bring out the dessert. Do you think everyone will have room?"

His weathered face split into a wide grin. "Oh yeah."

Minutes later when the men were devouring their dessert, Caleb strode into the kitchen.

He wasn't smiling and she couldn't read his somber expression. Maybe he hadn't liked the meal so much after all. Her mouth went dry. "Is everything all right?"

He nodded and offered her an almost apologetic smile, as if he were surprised himself at the quality of the meal. "More than all right. Half the men in there want to propose to you based on that meal alone. What did you season the chicken with?"

Emma soaked up the small compliment and fought the heat rushing to her cheeks. "It's a family secret, sorry."

"Everyone's pretty much finished so if you don't mind I'd like to introduce you to everyone."

"Uh, sure." She trailed behind him into the quiet room.

He kept a gentle grip on her upper arm as he rattled off names. It was hard to focus with him so close and holding her in such a possessive way. She didn't think he meant anything by it, but it felt strange. She resisted the urge to pull her arm away. It was crazy but her heart beat such a staccato tattoo against her rib cage she feared he could somehow hear it. As soon as he finished, the men stood and started clearing the table.

"Please leave everything, you don't have to—"

Caleb's grip tightened. Not painfully but the pressure on her arm increased. He took a small step back out of the way so that she had no choice but to follow. In single file, the men strode out of the dining room like a parade of mimes. She winced when she heard the clanging sounds of them dropping the china into the sink.

When the last man had gone, she looked up at Caleb in confusion. Before she could question, he answered. "Since it's your first night and you look ready to fall asleep on your feet I told the men to clear the table and I'll be doing the dishes."

She opened her mouth to protest but he shook his head. "This is probably the only time I'll do this so take advantage—unless of course you make dessert like that again." Without waiting for her response, he strode into the kitchen and started shoving plates into the dishwasher. Again she cringed. Even if he did have a tight butt and forearms to drool over, he was like the proverbial bull in a china closet. No grace or finesse.

Part of her wanted to argue but the part with the tired feet and droopy eyes let him win. "Okay."

She started for the hallway but turned at the door. "I've got the quiches in the fridge. I'll need to pop them in the oven in the morning. What time is breakfast?"

"Seven." He didn't glance up, just continued shoving dishes into the machine.

Twenty minutes later, Emma stood under the pulsing rhythm of the shower, letting the jets massage her aching body until the water turned chilly and forced her to get out. Not bothering to blow-dry her hair she smoothed vanilla lotion on her legs and slipped on yoga pants and a spaghetti strap top before slipping between the cool, cotton sheets. After setting the digital alarm, she finally let herself relax. Tomorrow was a new day.

For the first time in eight years, she felt safe. Completely and utterly safe. Sure, it had a lot to do with the rough looking man downstairs but that was okay. No one knew where she was and even if they did, she had a sneaking suspicion that Caleb slept with one eye open and a gun under his pillow anyway. She wondered if he slept in the nude too. The unexpected thought sent a jolt of awareness straight to her core. She shouldn't care one way or the other what he wore to bed. For all she knew he had a girlfriend.

No, she doubted it, because if she was his girlfriend, she wouldn't spend one night out of his bed. Any woman with a pulse would have to be crazy to leave him alone. She hadn't even given him her real last name and she was fantasizing about going to bed with him.

She groaned and buried her face in one of the pillows when a soft knock on the door jerked her back to reality. Panic clutched her throat for a millisecond. An intruder wouldn't knock. It had to be Caleb. Clutching the sheet against her chest she called out, "Come in."

A second later Caleb's large frame filled the doorway. He stopped abruptly and stared at her, mouth partially open. She glanced down in confusion but nothing appeared out of place. All body parts were covered. "Is everything okay?"

He nodded and cleared his throat and whatever trance he'd been in, vanished. "I just wanted to let you know I left my company credit card on the kitchen counter in case you need to do any grocery shopping tomorrow," he mumbled, his voice barely audible above the sounds of her own breathing.

"Okay, thanks. Won't you be at breakfast tomorrow?"

"Probably not. I've got a meeting at the bank early tomorrow morning and I'm meeting with a breeder in

the afternoon so you probably won't see me until tomorrow night. If you need anything Robert will help
you. He's the one—"

She nodded and clutched the sheet a little higher. Despite his soft speech, he stared at her as if he'd like to eat
her whole. Damn her traitorous body, that thought
wasn't such a bad one. Involuntarily she clenched her
thighs together and swallowed, trying to ignore the heat
pooling between her legs. "I know which one he is.
Thanks."

He gave a slight nod, then shut the door behind him.
Why had he trusted her with his credit card? For all he
knew she'd just take it and run. She wouldn't, of course,
but for some reason that small act touched her.

She stared at the closed door for a few moments before burying her face in the pillow again. This could not
be happening. She was on the run from a maniac and
her hormones were going haywire. Clearly, she had is-
sues.

* * *

Caleb shifted uncomfortably as he shut the door behind him. For a moment he'd thought she'd been naked
under the sheet. But it had been a nude colored type of
top. Didn't seem to matter, the sight had kicked his fantasies into overdrive. She'd tried to hide herself but the

nightlight next to her bed cast a soft, amber glow around her, shining right through the thin sheet. Illuminating her small, pert breasts perfectly even through the top. Her nipples had been rock hard underneath the sheer material.

He couldn't live under the same roof as her and not go insane. He'd thought her beautiful before but sitting in bed with wet, dark hair cascading around her heart shaped face, no makeup, she looked like a goddess. A goddess with huge, guarded eyes waiting for him. Only for him. He'd seen the appreciative glances from his men tonight so more than likely he would make an announcement tomorrow. She was off limits.

CHAPTER FOUR

Breakfast had been ridiculously easy and the cleanup even easier. Out of the three large dishes, there hadn't been one scrap of quiche left. It was as if they'd literally licked the plates clean. Her pride swelled a little but she had a feeling that after a month of Caleb's cooking, they'd be grateful for anything half-way decent she threw in front of them. The ravenous grunts she'd heard earlier were a good indication that Caleb would want to keep her around. Which is exactly what she'd been counting on. At least until she could figure out who she could trust.

After she loaded the dishwasher, she started an over-sized load of laundry, then dusted the entire downstairs. She didn't venture into Caleb's room because she wasn't sure if that would be invading his privacy too much. Considering he was a bachelor, she was surprised the house wasn't a complete mess. Besides the kitchen and dining room, his office was the only room actually lived in, but other than dusting it and emptying the wastebas-ket, it was already clean. The formal living room, the den, and the two downstairs bathrooms looked basically untouched except for a thin layer of dust over the lamps, wooden slat blinds and other furniture. She planned to vacuum the rugs later, but first she had some errands to run. At least she managed to start a second load of laundry and put the first load in the dryer before she left. How Caleb managed to let his clothes pile up for so long was beyond her.

February in Florida was an unusually chilly month for the sunshine state and as she'd come to realize, it was even colder the farther north and farther away from Miami she'd driven. Remembering the frantic rush she'd been in when packing, it was a wonder she'd been able to bring as much stuff as she had. She shrugged on a camel-colored, belted, wool coat, locked up the house with the key Caleb had left for her and went in search of her truck. It wasn't where she'd left it so she ventured toward the stables.

Male voices grew louder the closer she got to the huge barn so she knew she was headed in the right direction. Although she heard voices, she wasn't exactly sure how to get inside. After passing six closed Dutch-style doors along the side of the barn she found the entrance.

Once inside, she realized that the closed doors from the outside were individual stables and they all had horses inside. Her boots crunched over the wooden planks and dirt as she passed bales of hay and strange looking machinery. Emma tried to ignore the snorting animals and smell of fresh forage. It wasn't necessarily a bad odor, just different from what she was used to.

She continued toward the end of the long stable but jerked to a halt before rounding the corner when she heard her name.

"I'd definitely hit it," one said.

"I'd do her for her cooking skills alone," another said.

"Yeah, I'd like to bend her over the kitchen table and..." whoever was talking stopped and she could just imagine the rude hand gestures he was making.

"I don't know guys, I think Caleb might have something to say about that. Did you see the way he dressed up for dinner last night?"

They all started laughing, so she pivoted on her heels, afraid to hear more and hurried back in the direction she'd come. She'd find her truck on her own. Just as she stepped back out of the barn and into the fresh air, she slammed into a broad chest. Gentle hands steadied her and she found herself staring into Robert's concerned eyes.

"You all right hon? What're you doing out here?" His slow, soothing, southern drawl was just as relaxed as the way he walked.

"I'm just looking for my truck," she mumbled. She could feel heat creeping up her neck and face at the men's crude remarks. It wasn't that she'd never heard men talk like that before—Ricardo's men were disgusting pigs—but she'd never been the object of discussion. At least not that she knew of. Back home no one would have had the guts to talk about her that way, even if they knew the truth about her and Ricardo. It was all about pretense.

He opened his mouth as if to say something but evidently changed his mind and instead pointed out toward the pastures to what looked like an abandoned shed. "Caleb moved it last night but you might be better off taking mine for now, at least until one of us can look at it. I think you've got a problem with the transmission but I don't know for sure."

He didn't even know her and was willing to let her drive his vehicle? How's that for southern hospitality? "If you're sure you don't mind..."

"Of course not, come on, follow me."

She didn't feel right driving his vehicle but she didn't want to risk driving the truck she'd stolen before she left Miami unless it was absolutely necessary. Her brand new SLR McLaren Roadster still sat in the four-car garage back home but driving it hadn't been an option. That would have been like putting out a homing beacon with the GPS in it. She still felt guilty for taking something that wasn't hers, but when it came down to surviving, stealing from a stranger was the least of her worries.

She followed him to the opposite side of the barn to where four, dusty, F350s were parked all in a row. Driving the normal sized truck had been a feat in itself. She had no clue how she was going to steer one of those monsters.

"Mine's the gray one." He handed her the keys, tilted his black hat and strode back toward the barn quicker than she'd seen him move so far.

Okay then. She'd wanted to ask where the library was but figured it should be easy enough to find. Lake City wasn't exactly a bustling metropolis. Which is why she'd chosen it. She'd never heard of it, so chances were, Ricardo hadn't either. As long as she stayed under the radar she should be safe.

Despite all the dips and pot holes along the rugged country terrain, once she passed the main gate, the road evened out until she hit US-90. Finding the library proved to be simple. She just drove around the small town and looked for signs. Once inside the rectangular, one-story building, she received a few strange looks from the five patrons but she'd been expecting it. She was a stranger in a small town. At least no one stared exceptionally long though. She'd been worried about being recognized but after a few cursory glances, everyone seemed to go back to minding their own business.

In a tactical move, she chose a computer closest to a wall with a window. Even though she hadn't used her phone or any credit cards, she still wanted a view of any outside traffic. Google was her best ally right about now because she had no freaking clue how to go about what she needed to do next. She tried a multitude of search terms. *FBI, how to report a crime with the FBI, Florida FBI Division, report a crime in Florida.* Finally, a website for the Miami Division of the FBI popped up and what she found gave her hope. There was a page on how to report a crime and it included names and phone numbers.

Bingo! She jotted down everything in the small notebook she carried with her, dropped it in her purse and exited the library with as little fanfare as possible. She'd considered printing everything out but hadn't wanted to risk a nosy librarian seeing anything. *Stay invisible.* That was her new mantra for the next few weeks. Or until she found outside help.

She nearly tripped the second her boots hit the gravel parking lot. Caleb leaned casually against "her" truck, looking down at his cell phone. Keeping silent, she continued toward him until he finally noticed her. In the sunlight, she saw his hair was more auburn than brown and even though he'd combed it, a few unruly curls refused to stay in place, giving him an almost boyish look.

When he saw her, his mouth turned up slightly at the corners in what she assumed was his version of a smile. For some stupid reason, her heart rate sped up. Considerably.

Thankful for her dark sunglasses, she greedily drank in the sight of him, even though she knew she shouldn't.

Dressed in a multi-striped blue and black button-down dress shirt, no tie, a single button black blazer that screamed quality, he looked like a powerful, corporate raider instead of a rancher. Though she was loathe to admit it, if there was one thing she knew about more than anything, it was fashion. The suit he wore was almost certainly from the Versace collection. She'd bet her first week's pay on it. If she even made it a week.

He looked civilized. Almost.

Unsure of why he was waiting for her, she gave him a tight lipped smile and reined in her hormones.

"Hi?" It came out as a question. She knew she sounded rude but couldn't seem to help herself. Being near him put her on edge.

Caleb pushed up from his leaning position and stuck his hands in his pockets. He cleared his throat and she noticed his Adam's apple bob up and down. "Saw the truck and since I know Robert wouldn't be at the library, I figured it was you."

"I just wanted to check my email." She didn't need an excuse, what she did in her personal time was her business, but the words still managed to come out defensively. Great, now she was being rude to her boss. *Gah.*

He shrugged. "I actually wanted to see if you'd have lunch with me. My meeting ended early and I've got some time to kill before I meet with the breeder."

Beneath her shades, she felt her eyes widen and for the second time in thirty seconds, she was thankful for the protection they gave her. Having lunch with Caleb would mean making polite, small talk. Small talk would lead to personal questions and no matter how innocent they were, she'd still have to lie to him.

About who she was, where she came from and even who her family was. The thought of lying to him burned a crater in her stomach. Her entire life she'd glossed over her family history. For unknown reasons, she didn't want to gloss over anything for him.

She looked down at the pavement and cleared her throat. She felt bad because something told her he'd gone out on a limb asking her to lunch. "Uh, I can't . . . I've still got to buy groceries, do more laundry and run a few other errands and..."

"No, I understand, I-I'll see you tonight." He quickly retreated toward his truck and was out of the parking lot before she'd gotten her keys out of her purse.

* * *

Caleb kicked a rock out of his way and stalked to the house. Hours after he'd seen Emma and he still felt foolish. He cringed at the stupid words that had fallen from his mouth. He'd practically asked her, an employee, on a date and by the uncomfortable way she'd looked away from him, it was obvious she'd thought he was hitting on her.

He hadn't planned to ask her to lunch but he'd seen that truck and known it had to be her at the library. A glimpse; that was all he'd wanted of her. At least that's what he told himself. He shouldn't have stuck around to say hi but he couldn't seem to think with his head around her. The sight of that truck in the parking lot and his dick had gone on full alert. He didn't need this kind of distraction in his life.

He'd just avoid her. It was the only logical thing to do. One thing he knew for sure, she couldn't stay under the same roof. Not if he wanted to keep his sanity. As soon as he found someone to replace her, he'd let her go.

Right. He knew exactly how that would go over with his men.

Caleb jerked his head around at the sound of a loud crunching sound. Metal smashing against metal. "What the..."

He sprinted toward the main gate and nearly tripped. Robert's truck was wedged between two wooden posts. Barbed wire coiled around the front, stripping off huge chunks of paint. Though it didn't look like it would need any engine repair, it would definitely need a new paint job.

He shut the front door to the truck to silence the in-cessant dinging. Emma stood off to the side on a patch of grass shifting from one booted foot to the other. Her dark eyes were unnaturally wide and she chewed so hard on her bottom lip he was afraid she'd draw blood.

"Are you all right?"

She gave a jerky nod, then looked from him to the truck, then back again. Her delicate face pale, she twisted her hands in front of her stomach. "I don't know what happened. I'm not used to driving something so big."

He smothered a grin when he realized she wasn't hurt. How she'd managed to miss the main gate was beyond him. It was over two truck widths wide. He shook his head and rubbed a hand over his five o'clock stubble. Robert would be pissed but he'd get over it. "I just don't understand..."

"Well to be fair, all the damage isn't from the fence."

"What?" His head snapped to attention.

He wouldn't have thought it possible but her eyes grew even bigger. She opened her mouth but quickly snapped it shut.

"What happened Emma?"

She let out a silvery little laugh, laced with guilt and winced. "I also ran into a couple of shopping carts."

"Damn woman, is this your first time driving? What's the matter with you?"

Guilt and embarrassment disappeared fast. She put her hands on her slim hips and frowned at him, her dark eyes flashing to life. "*Nothing* is the matter with me! One of your stupid cows charged me and I panicked."

A cow charged her? He stared at her for a long, hard moment and tried to think of a retort but couldn't come up with anything that wouldn't offend her. Fighting a laugh, he cleared his throat. "Come on, I'll help you unload the groceries, then I'll take care of this later."

Emma nodded and he noted that she kept darting nervous glances around the land beyond the main yard and was never more than a hand span away from him. Not that he minded the closeness but he didn't want her fearful every time she ventured past the main house.

"The cows aren't going to hurt you Emma," he said as he handed her another brown paper bag. "Haven't you ever seen a farm animal before? Even at the zoo?"

She glanced up at him, as if she'd forgotten his existence, her face pinched and flushed pink. "What? Oh, no, I've never been to the zoo."

He frowned, but didn't respond. They managed to get all the bags inside in two trips. He'd never helped Rachel with groceries when she worked for him. To be fair, he'd also never wanted to pin Rachel flat on her back, fuck her until neither one of them could move, resurface to the real world for sustenance, then fuck some more.

Thoughts he should not be having about his employee.

Once he'd helped Emma inside the kitchen he tried to help unload the bags but she had other ideas. Every time he took something out of one of the bags, she plucked it from him his hands.

It didn't take long to figure out he was in her way, which should have been his hint to leave. Hell, this was her domain since she was taking over the new position and he had a shitload of work he could be doing, but . . . he found himself drawn to her.

When she muttered something about the pantry, he frowned and peered inside it. "What's wrong with the pantry?" Cans, boxes of pasta, cereal and other random dry foodstuff filled it. There wasn't much there but everything looked okay to him.

Her brows furrowed together and she gave a little head shake in his direction as if he'd grown horns. Unfortunately, that little head shake turned him on more than anything any woman had ever done. His cock stirred in his pants and his throat tightened as he stared down at her. Yeah, he was in serious trouble. And that was his cue to leave. He gave a quick excuse and backed out of the kitchen but before he'd made his exit, she stopped him.

"Caleb?"

"Yeah?" He pivoted in the doorway. When she said his name, his heart nearly jumped out of his chest.

"You look very nice today." Her eyes crinkled slightly and the corners of her lips curled up. Not into a full smile but he'd take what he could get.

"Thanks." He wasn't sure what else to say but she'd started bustling around the kitchen, ignoring his presence, so he assumed saying nothing would be the best response. If he did nothing, he was safe and he didn't run the risk of sticking his foot in his mouth. Once a day was quite enough, thank you.

In his room, he stripped out of the monkey suit his ex-fiancé had insisted he buy and changed back into comfortable jeans and a flannel work shirt. Just as he'd laced his work boots back up, his bedroom door swung open and Robert stormed in.

"What the hell happened to my truck?" His friend grabbed the door handle to stop it from ricocheting off the wall again.

Caleb inwardly groaned. He'd hoped to have this conversation later. "You can drive mine for now."

"I don't want yours, I want mine. What the hell happened?"

"I don't know."

"What do you mean you don't know?"

He shrugged. "Emma said a cow charged her."

All traces of anger disappeared from his friend's face. He cleared his throat once. "She said one of *our* cows charged her?"

He nodded and stood up. "Yep."

A grin split Robert's face wide open. "Well, hell."

"You haven't said anything to her about it have you?"

Robert shook his head. "Nah, I saw it and thought I'd talk to you first. I didn't want to say something stupid and scare off the best cook we've ever had. Especially after what happened earlier."

They left his room and headed down the long hall-way toward the kitchen. Already, delicious, if foreign, smells wafted through the house.

"Good, let's keep it that way. I'll pay for the damages..." He jerked to a halt when Robert's last comment registered. "What do you mean, after what happened earlier?"

Robert shoved his hands in his pockets and cleared his throat.

"What happened?"

"I think Emma might have overheard some of the new hands talking about her. I found her wandering around the stables today looking for her truck..."

He held up a hand and sighed. A detailed explanation wasn't necessary. He knew exactly how his men talked. Some of the new men were barely twenty, horny all the time and crude. Hell, he'd been exactly the same way at that age. "I'll take care of it later."

When they entered the kitchen, Emma was taking a casserole dish from the oven. She set it on the counter then glanced from Caleb to Robert and when her soft eyes landed on Robert, she winced. "I'm so sorry. I'll pay for whatever—"

"Don't worry about it. How 'bout you bake me an apple pie a week for the next month and we'll call it even?"

She blinked a few times then gave a heart-stopping smile. "Deal."

Caleb fought an irrational surge of jealousy. Robert was married. Happily married at that. Even so, he didn't want her looking at anyone like that but him. Which was just plain stupid.

He chanced one last glimpse of her before walking into the dining room. She wore jeans again today, low rise this time and they molded perfectly to her curves. When she bent over the stove, he got a fantastic view of her ass. Her brown wrap-around sweater rose up on her back, giving him not only a great view of her assets but a clear picture of the bottom half of a tattoo. It was too hard to tell what it was without lifting her shirt and... No, no, no.

CHAPTER FIVE

She'd set the table earlier in an attempt to establish a pattern. Caleb and Robert were the first two to show up so she wanted to get everything else out before the other men arrived. When she entered the dining room, she tried to ignore Caleb's gaze on her.

He wasn't outwardly leering but she could feel the intensity coming from his direction as if he was sending heat seeking missiles her way. She knew he wanted her. She might not have much experience with men but she knew when one was interested. And Caleb Ryder was. She'd recognized his attraction to her almost immediately but when he'd asked her to lunch earlier, there had been no mistaking the simmering heat in his eyes that practically screamed he was biding his time trying to bed her. He might not even be aware but his green eyes flashed a little brighter every time he saw her.

Oh, she wasn't worried about him doing something inappropriate but just knowing he wanted her set her a little on edge. And a lot on fire. Knowing he wanted her as much as she wanted him was not a piece of knowledge she needed right now. Why couldn't he hide it a little better?

He wasn't even her normal type. Not that she really had one but she'd never envisioned herself wanting a rough looking cowboy with tattoos. He wasn't conventionally attractive and he definitely wasn't a pretty boy, although he did have a boyish charm about him. That could have something to do with the beat-up brown cowboy hat he wore all the time and the way he mumbled around her. It was strange but she preferred him in his jeans and button-down flannels as opposed to the Versace suit he'd worn earlier.

Why had she told him he looked nice? She still wanted to kick herself for that comment. She couldn't remember ever being so attracted to a man. His hands were rough and calloused but something told her he'd be gentle if he touched her. She clenched her legs together and imagined him running his hands down her...

"Emma?" Caleb's deep voice interrupted her thoughts.

She looked up to find Robert and Caleb both looking at her and she realized she'd been staring off into space.

"I'm sorry, what?" How long had she been standing there, staring into the casserole? She fought the heat rushing to her cheeks. At least they couldn't read her thoughts.

"We just wanted to know what that was," he said, pointing at one of the dishes.

"Pierogi Casserole."

She received blank stares from both of them. Before either one could ask what was in it, everyone started filing in.

She escaped into the kitchen, knowing that Caleb would probably ask her to join them again. When she heard grunts of appreciation coming from the other room, she went to the utility room, took out the dry laundry, and started one last load before calling it a night. She grabbed a bottle of water from the fridge, the small salad she'd prepared earlier for herself and slipped up to her room. Eating in her room felt rude but she wanted to go over the notes she'd taken at the library and she couldn't do that in the kitchen.

In an hour, she would head back down and clean up the mess once everyone left. At least tomorrow was Saturday and she wouldn't have to worry about cooking in the morning. She'd spied a laptop in Caleb's office. Maybe he would let her use it.

She started reviewing her notes when a huge yawn escaped. Her feet ached and her eyes felt as if sandbags weighed them down. A little nap couldn't hurt. *I'll just close my eyes for a few minutes,* she thought.

* * *

Caleb lay in bed staring at the ceiling. Familiar shadows cast from the dim moonlight danced around his room. Crickets, frogs and even the horses were quiet tonight. The only sound audible was his breathing. Nonetheless, sleep was impossible. Not with the mysterious, sexy brunette one floor above him. After dinner he'd been worried about her, so he'd gone to check on her. He found her sound asleep, with one arm curled underneath her head on the small, antique desk, papers scattered everywhere and an untouched salad beside her.

There was no way he could have woken her up. She looked so peaceful, if a bit uncomfortable and disturbing her had seemed cruel. Besides, if he was going to wake her up, it certainly wasn't for something as mundane as doing the dishes. So, he'd done the dishes, cleaned up and now he was staring at the ceiling with a raging hard-on. It was ridiculous. He hadn't had any serious interest in sex in a year. Not since he found his ex-fiancé fucking two of his men. And if he was completely honest, he hadn't had any interest—at least not in her—a solid six months before that. The relationship had died and he'd been too stubborn, or lazy to admit it.

Now all Emma had to do was walk into the room and he was ready to go. She didn't even have to look at him. Although when she turned those guarded eyes his way, that made it worse. And her sweet scent permeated everything. It wasn't overt or overbearing but subtle enough so when he entered the kitchen or walked down the hallway, she enveloped him.

He rolled over, glanced at the digital clock on his nightstand and groaned. Midnight. Whiskey was the only thing that might help. He slipped on a pair of boxers and went to his study. Just as he set the decanter down, a crash sounded from the kitchen.

On instinct he grabbed one of the pistols from the desk drawer. He had a weapon in his room and one in the study for practical reasons. The probability of anyone penetrating his security system was slim but he hadn't heard Emma stir upstairs so he wasn't taking any chances.

His feet were silent along the pine hardwood floor in the hallway. His heartbeat slowed the closer he came to the archway leading to the kitchen. Training kicked in and he scanned the kitchen in one quick sweep. Ice chilled his veins at her slight silhouette in the pantry door. He immediately lowered his weapon.

Emma's eyes widened in horror, she dropped the wine bottle in her hand and let out a scream that pierced his soul. Glass and crimson liquid spewed across the floor. He twisted the dimmer switch so that light flooded the room and stepped into the kitchen but stopped short when Emma flinched and retreated further into the pantry. Away from him and away from the broken glass.

"Are you okay?" he asked, weapon still in hand.

"I'm fine. It was dark and I couldn't find the light switch. I crashed into one of the chairs before I figured out how to turn on the light. Sorry I woke you." She cringed and glanced down at the glass in front of her.

"Don't move," he ordered before disappearing. He didn't want her getting hurt. Seconds later, he was back wearing boots. Thankful she still stood where he'd left her, he placed his pistol on the small table by the entry-way before he walked toward her.

His shoes crunched over the broken pieces but she didn't pull away as he lifted her up and carried her to the counter, even if her dark eyes were wide and frightened. He knew he'd scared her but she wasn't saying anything and that scared him more than if she would have started yelling at him.

"Let me clean this up and we'll talk. Okay?"

She nodded in agreement but he didn't miss her eyes flit to where he'd laid the gun across the room on the table where he kept his mail. After what felt like an eternity, he'd swept up the glass, the wine and run a wet cloth over the floor to pick up any excess shards.

"I woke up and realized what time it was. I came down to clean up but it was already taken care of and I couldn't go back to sleep. I thought a glass of wine might help." She still watched him warily, and her voice sounded small in the quiet of the room.

He fought the twinge of guilt twisting up his stomach for pointing a weapon at her. It wasn't as if he'd done it intentionally but he felt it nonetheless. He wouldn't blame her if she packed up and left in the middle of the night.

He shook his head and rubbed a hand over his face. "I had the same idea. I'm sorry, I heard the crash and... God, I'm sorry for scaring you."

She let out a shaky laugh and he could see some of her earlier fear ebb away. But not by much. "I'm just sorry you had to do the dishes tonight. Again. I'm feeling like the worst employee ever right about now."

He snorted at that. "You've cooked some of the best meals we've had in ages so I wouldn't go that far. Look, let's just forget about tonight. We're both getting used to sharing the house."

"Okay." The word came out breathy and seductive, though he doubted she even realized it. Just as she probably didn't realize how utterly adorable she looked sitting there in a long john thermal pajama set.

He'd never thought of long johns as sexy in any way but hers were unlike any he'd seen. Pink and yellow kisses on a black background covered the clingy material that molded to her entire body like a second skin. She wasn't wearing a bra and he could see the outline of her nipples perfectly. They were rock hard, from the cold, or more probably, from the adrenaline rush at having a gun pointed at her. He'd seen it more times than he could count in battle. Most men he knew were horny after a firefight or a near miss with death. Biology. Plain and simple. Women were built the same way.

He averted his gaze to find her staring at him, eyebrows pulled together. Some unfathomable expression shrouded her pretty face. Desire or fear? Impossible to tell. Maybe both.

"Come on, I think I've got an old bottle of cabernet in my study." The counter wasn't that high. She could have gotten down by herself but he wanted to feel her body against his again. If just for a moment.

Before she could move, he was in front of her. He hooked his hands under her arms and picked her up again. "In case there are any little pieces of glass I missed, I don't want you getting cut," he murmured in her ear. Too close. Way too close but he couldn't help himself. Vanilla and some other exotic scent tickled his nose.

The walk across the kitchen to the entryway was a short one and she couldn't weigh more than one hundred ten pounds, though he doubted even that. He set her down on the wooden floor but didn't take a step back like he knew he should. Instead, his hands drifted down to her slim waist. He didn't pull her closer. He didn't make a move at all. Just kept his hands there, watching her. Waiting for a reaction. Any reaction.

She didn't move either but her face was unreadable. No repulsion. No desire. Nothing. She didn't pull back or step forward. Just stared at him, searching his face for something. The tick of the clock from the kitchen and their shallow breathing was the only sound penetrating the quiet night air. It was as if a heavy blanket had settled around the house, enveloping them. Streams of moonlight illuminated the hallway and other rooms through random slivers and window openings throughout the house.

When she leaned forward, he didn't stop to second guess what they were about to do. Before he could change his mind, he pulled her against him and slanted his mouth over hers. He needed to taste her like he needed his next breath. He explored gently with his tongue and when she moaned into his mouth, he deepened his probing. She wrapped her hands around his neck, gripping him as if she was afraid he'd leave her. Something he couldn't do now, not if someone held a gun to his head.

Her hair cascaded down her back, around her face and he wondered what it would feel like to have that hair surround him as she rode him. He jerked at the image in his head and his cock surged up against her. With one hand, he cupped the back of her head, fisting her thick hair through his fingers. If he didn't stop soon, he was likely to take her on the floor and she deserved better.

Somehow, he managed to extricate his mouth from hers. He pulled his head back. Her lips were swollen and moist and her eyes were heavy with desire.

"Do you want to stop?" He wasn't sure if it would be better if she said yes or no. This was stupid. Beyond stupid. But damn, he wanted her to say yes.

In jerky motions, she shook her head. They needed to get to his bedroom. Fast. Without asking her, he picked her up, carried her as if she was a weightless doll and didn't stop until they were at the foot of his bed.

There were too many reasons to count why he shouldn't be doing this and one very good reason he should. He didn't know much about her except that she was scared and on the run.

They stood toe to toe and in her bare feet, she came to the middle of his chest. He stared down at her, gauging her expression and watching the rapid rise and fall of her breasts. "Is this what you want Emma?"

She smiled. Not a full one but her perfect pink lips curled up invitingly and her dark eyes flashed to life. "Yes."

One word. That's all he needed to hear. Despite her answer, she still looked a little nervous. Hell, so was he. Take it slowly. That had become his new mantra. Slow and easy. Something told him she didn't fuck hard and fast. Even though that's all he could think of doing, he knew it wouldn't be right for her. At least not their first time. She would need to trust him.

With one hand, he cupped the back of her head and picked up where he'd left off. She tasted just as good as she smelled. Sweet, inviting and utterly feminine.

CHAPTER SIX

Emma was trembling. Maybe not on the outside but her insides felt like Jell-O. If Caleb hadn't been holding her steady, she'd have collapsed at the knees by now. At least she had a bed behind her. She was surprised he hadn't already started stripping her clothes off. He'd seemed almost on edge before, ready to pounce, but apparently she was wrong because he was taking his time with her. Making sure she was comfortable. Something she was incredibly thankful for.

He held the back of her head gently with one hand and with his other, he pulled her tight against him, his hold firm and steadying. His erection strained against his boxers and was pushing against her stomach. Too many emotions swirled inside for her to make a move. She felt as if she was clutching on to him for dear life. In a way she was.

Only a few days had passed since she'd left but she felt like she'd been running from her past and who she was her entire existence. She'd never opened herself up to anyone because of fear. Fear of the consequences.

Not now. Now, nothing could stop her. She deserved a little bliss right? And being with Caleb *was* absolutely right. His large hands rested on her body but he didn't make a move to take it to the next step.

She wasn't waiting for him any longer. This was happening. Without giving him any warning, she backed out of his embrace and pulled her thermal top off. Though they were inside, the cool night air rushed over her exposed body and she involuntarily shivered.

It could have been from the cold but it was more from the feral look he raked over her body. The room was dark, save for a small stream of light coming through the partially opened bathroom door. It illuminated Caleb, so that she could observe his expression. His green eyes looked almost black and his jaw twitched uncontrollably. The only thing she saw on his face was desire. She'd been admired before but she'd never been on the receiving end of such raw lust.

He still hadn't made a move to kiss her again though. His erection was real, very real but maybe he was having doubts.

Somehow, she found her voice, though the question came out as a whisper. "Do you want...is this what you want?"

He nodded and swallowed so hard she could see his Adam's apple bob up and down. "Yep."

She loved how succinct he could be. Well, she could be too. "Good."

His entire demeanor changed at that word. It wasn't his stance so much as the wild gleam in his eyes. No longer was he the calm and collected cowboy. Now, he was a predator. And she was his prey.

Something she found wildly erotic.

He pulled her roughly against him so that their naked chests collided. His muscled, slightly hairy chest rubbed against her already hard nipples, turning her on even more. His kissing alone had sent shock waves straight to her core, something she hadn't known was possible but the tortuous rhythmic motion of his body against hers was driving her hormones haywire.

Before she realized what was happening, he laid her on the bed and had shucked his boxers. He pulled a condom from the nightstand and faster than she would have imagined, he sheathed himself. Next time, if there was one, she wanted to put it on him.

She only had a moment to appreciate him in all his glory but it was long enough to admire his broad, muscular shoulders and chest. He didn't look like the gym rats she associated with back home. Most of the men she knew waxed and shaved any and all body hair and spent hours in the gym.

Not Caleb. He had a thatch of dark hair covering his chest but not so much that he looked like a rug, and his body was carved from hours of working outdoors. She was sure of it. In the pale light, he reminded her of a barbaric warrior. Random scars and nicks tattooed his entire body. And a couple of real tattoos. Instead of being turned off, she sucked in a breath and tried to steady her increasing heartbeat. She briefly wondered how he'd gotten all his wounds but dismissed her thoughts when he stretched out on top of her.

Crimson sheets cooled her backside, though nothing could cool the rest of her body. She was propped up against two of the pillows, almost in a sitting position, resisting the urge to squirm under his intense scrutiny.

He stared down at her as if she were a goddess. Lust rolled off him in waves and maybe it was her imagination but she could almost swear she smelled his desire, it was so potent. When he stretched his body over hers, he paid particular attention to her breasts. They weren't very impressive but he feasted on them as if he'd never seen a naked woman. He teased and tugged with his teeth, pulling moan after moan from her. She arched her head back against the pillow and pushed deeper into his mouth.

Involuntarily, she squeezed her legs together in a vain attempt to ease the ache but he gently nudged them back open with one of his thighs and peeled her long johns and panties off. Then with a free hand, he opened the sensitive folds and began rubbing her clit in such a slow, tortuous motion, her hips bucked wildly. He placed a firm hand over her stomach, momentarily stilling her.

One finger, then two slipped inside her and she moaned at the intrusion. He pushed deeper, deeper—and froze. He lifted his head back, watching her face carefully, but didn't withdraw.

"You're a virgin." He wasn't asking.

She'd been hoping he wouldn't be able to tell. She'd played enough sports in high school, she went scuba diving all the time and hell, she was twenty-six. She knew about sex. Knew all the basics. The probability of her hymen being intact was slim. Apparently not slim enough.

She swallowed hard and prayed he wouldn't stop now. "Yes, I am but hopefully I won't be after tonight." There, she'd said it. Now it was up to him to decide because she wanted this.

He might think it strange that a woman of her age was still a virgin but he also knew nothing about her life. Growing up, no one had wanted to touch Javier Garcia's daughter. Well, they might have wanted to but nobody in their right mind wanted to get involved with an arms dealer's daughter. Not if they wanted to live. And the ones who did were creeps anyway. Then, after her father's death, his protégé, Ricardo Mendez had blackmailed her into being his girlfriend for one stupid reason.

So, yeah, she might be a virgin but only because the opportunity hadn't presented itself. If Caleb backed out now, she just might die of embarrassment. Or kill him. She couldn't decide.

CHAPTER SEVEN

Emma was a virgin. A fucking virgin. How was that even possible? Every cell and fiber in his body screamed at him to back off. Leave her alone. He never would have known if he hadn't decided to test her slickness before thrusting into her. Now he almost wished he hadn't.

Almost.

She stared at him but her dark eyes were no longer filled with lust and desire but uncertainty and a small measure of fear. His chest clenched. A gentleman would stop. A gentleman would take his hands off her, put his clothes back on and tuck her into bed for the night.

But, he was no gentleman and he had no intention of leaving her.

He didn't understand how someone as gorgeous and sweet as Emma was still a virgin. He also didn't give a shit. She'd chosen him. Emma, the most beautiful woman he'd ever laid eyes on had chosen him as her first. Possessiveness like he'd never known overwhelmed him.

Without a word, he resumed stroking her clit with his thumb and slowly moved his fingers inside her tight body. As he probed and primed her, he watched her face. Just watched. Some of her doubt vanished and a small dose of confidence was back, glittering in her eyes.

All thoughts and fantasies of fucking for hours disappeared. He had no experience with virgins but he had a feeling she was going to be sore afterward. Why she'd decided that tonight was the night and with him of all people, he couldn't imagine. He did know he was going to make this good for her. Especially if he wanted a repeat performance.

Everything about her looked delicate, from her petite build to the satiny pink folds between her legs. She writhed every time he touched her and that worried him a little. He hadn't had sex in so long and now his body was primed for an all-day marathon. He didn't want to hurt her when he finally got inside her.

"Do you like this?" he whispered against her ear.

Her cheek rubbed against his as her head bobbed up and down. He dropped kisses along her jaw and neck until he located the sensitive spot below her ear. She nearly jumped off the bed when he raked his teeth over her skin.

"I guess you like that too."

A light laugh escaped and he felt some of the tension leave her body when her tight sheath loosened around his fingers. Maybe she'd been subconsciously holding her breath but soon after his lighthearted comment, her entire body released and relaxed underneath his. Her legs loosened and he knew she was close to climaxing. She just hadn't been allowing herself to let go until now.

Her breathing came in shallow gasps and her inner muscles began contracting around his two fingers, milking him in quicker successions. Without warning, she surged into orgasm.

"Oh my God." Her voice was hoarse, scratchy and he realized she was trying to hold on to some of the last shreds of her control.

He knew he needed to enter her while she was still climaxing. He poised himself at her entrance and even though she was climaxing, she understood what he was silently asking.

She nodded. "Yes, yes. Now."

With one long thrust he pushed inside her. Her eyes glazed over and she let out a sharp cry but just as quickly she focused on his face.

He held her gaze and began thrusting in long, hard strokes. He tried to hold himself back from pushing too deep but she'd wrapped her toned legs around his waist, urging him on, pulling him to the hilt. Instead of kissing her, he watched her. He wanted her to see his face when he came. Just as he'd seen hers.

She raked her hands and fingers over his chest and he lost it. The feel of her hands on his body was too much. He exploded without warning, coming just as quickly as she had. He kept pumping inside her for what felt like forever, until he was completely spent. She'd taken everything from him. He collapsed but rolled slightly to the side so he wouldn't suffocate her.

A million questions raced through his head but none of them mattered until Emma's needs were taken care of.

"That was amazing." She half turned toward him, a soft smile on her face.

That had to be a good sign. He'd expected a few tears. Instead, she was staring at him with a sweet, sated expression.

"Hold that thought." He dropped a light kiss on her forehead and left her splayed on the bed like some pagan offering.

In the bathroom, he wetted down two washcloths and discarded the condom. A slightly archaic sensation welled up inside him at the sight of her blood. He'd never thought of himself as a particularly primal being, but for the first time in his life, he understood why medieval men had hung bloody sheets from their windows. Apparently he wasn't as civilized as he thought.

He walked back into the bedroom, unsure of what kind of reaction to expect. Emma had pulled the sheet over her chest, not that it did much good. He could see her form outlined perfectly under the thin material.

Even if he couldn't, he had her entire body committed to memory.

He sat on the edge of the bed and held up the wash-cloth. "Do you mind?"

When she shook her head, he pulled the sheet down and gently wiped between her legs. Softly, reverently, afraid he'd hurt her. She lay back on the pillow and sighed in what sounded like appreciation. He laid the cloth on the nightstand and tried to gather his thoughts.

"Listen, honey, we need to talk. How is it possible that..."

"Does it matter?" she answered his unfinished question.

He was still curious how she'd been a virgin, but she was right. It didn't matter. The only thing that mattered was that she was with him right then. His cock, which had been at half mast, lengthened again as she stretched her body against his. Tough shit for him. She wasn't anywhere near ready to go again. But she would be tomorrow. Thank God tomorrow was Saturday. He had a few things to take care of but it wasn't going to happen. One of his men could cover for him.

He'd been ruthlessly driving himself for the past five years and he was taking the time to enjoy the beautiful woman who had literally fallen into his path.

He wrapped his arms around her, pulling her half on top of him. A few minutes later, the steady rise and fall of her chest was the only sign she was alive. Her breathing was so light he could barely hear anything else above the sound of his own erratic heartbeat.

He stared at the ceiling, knowing it was useless to try to sleep. She'd thrown a satiny leg over his lower body, the sensation of her covering him too much. He inwardly groaned and ran a hand through her long dark hair, caressing her back. Morning couldn't come soon enough.

* * *

Blood. Too much blood. Crimson pools expanded around their lifeless bodies and two pairs of dead eyes stared right at her. Through her. Judging her. Biting her knuckles, she held back a scream. She mustn't make a sound.

Before she could move from her hiding place, he turned and saw her peeking through the window of the pool house. His eyes turned red, like the devil. Out of the corner of her eyes, she saw the gleaming knife in his hand but she couldn't tear her gaze away from his glowing eyes. She opened her mouth to scream but no sound would come.

She was going to die.

"Emma. Emma, honey, wake up."

Blackness twisted her thoughts but when she opened her eyes, Caleb stared down at her, concern etched in every inch of his handsome face.

It had been a dream. Everything had just been a dream. Ricardo hadn't seen her and she was still alive.

"I'm sorry," she muttered and sat up.

Beads of sweat trickled down her back but she didn't shrug off Caleb's tight grip on her shoulders. His touch somehow grounded her and that's what she needed when it felt her heart would jump from her chest.

She wrapped her arms around her knees and put her head down. Caleb didn't speak as he rubbed her back in soothing rhythmic motions. Visions of blood and carnage clawed at her brain. She wished the images would just leave her alone. She wished . . . She wished a lot of things about her life were different, including where she came from. If her father hadn't been such a scumbag, she might have ended up differently. She might even have been married and had kids by now. Like a normal person.

"Do you feel like talking about it?" Caleb's deep voice brought her back to reality.

She lifted her head and turned to look at him. Over the years, she'd gotten pretty good at weeding out bullshitters. Being the daughter of a man who lied with practically every breath had its advantages. She might not be able to read Caleb most of the time but the concern in his voice and in his piercing eyes, was very real.

She wanted to tell him everything but if he knew who she was he'd probably send her packing. For once in her life, she decided to be selfish. She wanted to enjoy everything about him before she had to leave.

"No, I just had a stupid dream, that's all." She twisted from her current position to face him.

She felt exposed and a little strange sitting naked in front of him but he didn't seem to mind. In fact, he was completely hard. Her eyes widened and she swallowed so loudly she was sure he'd heard her.

"Oh." He sat in the same position as her so that their knees touched. His hard length was still as big—maybe bigger—than last night. It lengthened, pulsing, as if it had a life of its own. How had it ever fit inside her?

"Don't worry, it's been like that since you went to sleep." She tore her eyes away and forced herself to meet his gaze. A wry smile pulled at the corners of his mouth.

"You can't be serious," she gasped.

His small smile fell, belying the truth.

"Is that normal?" She inwardly cringed as soon as she asked the question. She didn't want him to think she was criticizing him in any way. Especially not after last night.

Instead of being offended, he chuckled. "No but ever since I laid eyes on you it seems to be a permanent condition. For better or worse."

"Maybe we should do something about it then." *Where had that come from?*

His eyes widened at her words. Hell, she was a little surprised at herself but her time was limited and she wanted to soak up as much of Caleb as she could.

"Maybe we should." He leaned forward and covered her mouth with his. His tongue traced her sensitive lips, biting and licking but he pulled away and stood just as she leaned in for more.

"What are you doing?"

"Wait here. For one second." He grabbed a condom from his nightstand, pivoted and disappeared through the bathroom door. Seconds later, she heard the sound of running water and understood what his intentions were. He appeared in the doorway, silhouetted by the bright light and her stomach lurched. He really was a perfect specimen of man. All steel muscle. Not an inch of fat anywhere on that lean form.

Momentary panic clutched her throat. Being naked in his bedroom, with barely any light at all was one thing but being naked with him under the bright lights beckoning from the other room was something else entirely. She swallowed her hesitation and walked toward him. The woodsy, spicy, male scent that was all Caleb enveloped her the moment her feet came in contact with the cool tile.

The bathroom was definitely masculine. No frilly hand towels, decorative soaps, or scented candles. Neutral sage green walls, a chocolate brown throw rug and matching striped green-and-brown towels hung from the towel rack. An electric razor sitting by one of the two sinks was the only sign that he actually used the bathroom. Steam had risen from the walk-in shower, covering the elongated mirror in a hazy mist and for that, she was thankful. She was nervous enough about Caleb seeing her naked. The thought of seeing them entwined together brought heat to her cheeks.

"Are you okay?" Caleb's deep voice grounded her.

"Yes." Oh yeah, she was just fine. If Caleb did to her what he did last night, she'd be more than okay.

Her body was a little sore but nothing could override the pleasure she knew she'd experience. He led her to the shower but instead of immediately jumping her, as she'd expected—and kind of hoped—he positioned her under the bursting jet streams. The hot water massaged her head, neck, shoulders and back. He stood back for a moment and in the bright light, she got a full close up of his lean form.

"So what's the story behind the butterfly tattoo on your back?"

His question took her off guard, but she shrugged. "I got it in college on Spring Break my sophomore year. It doesn't mean anything." That wasn't exactly true, but she wasn't planning to spill her guts to him anytime soon. He could just think it was a silly, meaningless tattoo. She'd gotten it as a tiny symbol to remind herself that she wouldn't always be under Ricardo's thumb. That she'd eventually get her freedom.

And now she had, even if it might only be for a little while.

She was thankful he didn't ask any more questions. Instead, Caleb lathered up a washcloth and began systematically washing her arms, her breasts, her stomach and when he reached between her legs, she couldn't take her eyes off the picture they made.

He was so much bigger and more powerful than she was, yet he handled her with such gentleness and delicacy that a strange lump settled in her throat. His cheekbones were flushed under his tanned skin as he slowly and deliberately stroked between her legs again. The soft material of the cloth and his reverent stroking lit her entire body on fire. It took a moment for her to realize he was watching her every expression as he touched her. She'd been so focused on his rough hands that she hadn't been paying attention to his face.

Without saying a word but keeping his gaze fixed on hers, he placed the cloth on the built-in bench. Before she could guess what he had planned, he leaned forward and licked her clit. Involuntarily she tried to take a step back but he gripped both of her thighs and continued torturing her with his tongue. Heat and moisture pooled between her legs and she knew he must be able to taste her wetness.

She ran her fingers through his soaked hair and gripped his head for support. She was going to come before he'd even gotten inside her. Rivulets of water ran down her chest and his back, creating ribbons and streams along both their bodies. It was the most sensuous thing she'd ever seen. A hot man between her legs, pleasuring her, wanting her for her, not what she could do for him or his career.

That thought alone almost sent her over the edge. A low, guttural moan sounded from somewhere deep inside her. Somewhere she hadn't known existed. She was so close to climaxing she almost hurt.

But, Caleb had other plans. "Not yet sweetheart. I want to be in you when you come."

He stood and joined her under the waterfall, dropping kisses on her forehead, cheeks, nose and everywhere in between. Her inner walls clenched, waiting for him but he seemed bent on torturing her. It took all her control not to beg him to thrust into her. She decided to take the initiative and ripped open the condom he'd brought. Putting one on a man was something foreign, but she found she enjoyed rolling it over his hard length.

When she was finished, her hands and fingers traced the scars along his chest and shoulders as he reached for something behind her. "Where did you get all these? From riding horses?"

Laughing lightly, he shook his head as he poured shampoo into his hands. "Turn around."

"You didn't answer me," she said as she turned her back to him.

"Honey, I don't ride horses for a living. I'm a breeder. I raise and sell thoroughbreds, cattle, poultry and anything else you can think of. In the winter, I open up part of my land for wilderness survival training to a couple of law enforcement agencies around the state. I also open up a limited section of my land for trail riding and equestrian training. I don't like to keep all my eggs in one basket so to speak."

Law enforcement? That was interesting. "Are you being deliberately obtuse? How did you get those scars?"

It was hard to concentrate with his erection pressed up against her back and him massaging her temple.

"I was in the Marines."

Ah. That would account for the menagerie of tattoos. Especially the one on his butt. She giggled at the thought of the tiny rose on his right cheek. It was so out of place on his hard body.

"That's funny why?" His hands fell and his voice had taken on a distinctive defensive note.

She turned to face him, letting the water wash the suds from her hair. She resisted the urge to smile at his down turned mouth. "I wasn't laughing at that, I was just thinking that must be when you got that adorable little tattoo on your butt. It seems so out of place compared to the tribal designs on your arm and the Celtic symbols on your back."

Caleb's face reddened. She blinked once to make sure she wasn't seeing things. He was actually embarrassed. "Yeah. I lost a bet," he mumbled and cleared his throat.

She reached her hands around his body and gripped his backside, pulling him against her. She loved the feel of his skin against hers. Since she had to look up to see him, she propped her chin on his chest and grinned up at his scowling face. "I think it's cute. In fact, I think it's so adorable, I'll need to further inspect it."

Her hands tightened on him and she dug her fingernails into his skin. Skin that should've been a little soft but was just as firm as the rest of his body. Taut muscles clenched under her grip and his eyes darkened aggressively.

Her inner walls clenched when he ran his hands down her hips and his mouth descended on hers. Good. She was more than ready to feel him inside her again. He hungrily ate at her mouth and backed her up against the wall. His hands gripped her hips so tightly she was sure to have bruises. Not that she minded. Not one tiny bit.

He lifted her against the wall and she wrapped her legs around his lean waist. The cool tile against her back was at odds with the steam from the shower and the heat flowing through her veins. Rough hands cupped her behind.

"You're so fucking beautiful," he murmured as he nipped her neck with his teeth.

Not exactly the poetry she'd dreamed of but his words turned her on more than she ever could have imagined because they came from him. He thought she was beautiful.

CHAPTER EIGHT

Caleb had no finesse. He knew that. He'd never cared before. Now he just wished he had some words other than "you're so fucking beautiful" to convey to Emma how he felt. Thankfully, she didn't seem to mind his crude language. If anything, her grip on his ass increased.

With a sudden thrust, he pushed inside her. She wrapped her legs around him even tighter as he pushed up and stilled. She was tight, probably a little sore but she was so damn wet. He'd done a good job of priming her earlier with his tongue, when all he'd wanted to do was drive into her. Everything about Emma was so soft and inviting. And she tasted so sweet.

She loved it when he sucked her nipples so he held still, completely embedded inside her and teased her. He made love to her breasts just as he'd done to her clit—delicately. He watched in fascination as her nipples pebbled to rocks under his caresses. Her long, dark hair cascaded down both sides of her breasts and along her arms. If he'd thought she'd been his fantasy when she'd first stepped onto his property, he now knew how wrong he was. This was so much better than fantasy. Emma was his living, breathing reality.

Her body writhed against his and in small circular motions, she moved up and down on his cock. He didn't shift from his position. He understood that she was rubbing her clit against him, even if she didn't fully know it herself.

Where had she been his whole life? Before his ex had left him and before her, sex had been a regular part of his life but it hadn't been something he couldn't live without. If a woman was around and willing, he'd been obliging. If not, his fist had always worked fine. Now, he couldn't imagine Emma not in his bed. Not riding him. Not there when he woke up.

This was only the second time they'd fucked and he was thinking of the future? Man, she was messing with his head.

He tore his mouth away from her breasts to look at her. Her eyes were closed, her head against the wall and her perfect lips were half open, inviting him. He centered right on her mouth. He needed to taste her. She moaned and without warning, her inner walls started contracting around him. Little contractions turned into big ones, drawing him deeper and tighter.

His chest rubbed against her soft skin, the simple motion intensified tenfold as he gripped her hips and began thrusting. He pounded so hard he was afraid he'd hurt her but she just moaned and writhed underneath him. And just like that, he came too, long and hard as he found his release.

When he was through, he laid his forehead against hers. He cupped her chin with one of his hands but didn't utter a word. He didn't want to say anything to screw up the moment. Both of their breathing was erratic and he could feel her staccato heartbeat. The running water had long since turned tepid. Not quite icy but he knew it wouldn't be long until it did.

She loosened her legs and he slackened his grip on her, letting her stand.

"Wow." She found her balance, a secretive smile playing across her lips.

Even though he should be completely sated, he knew it wouldn't take him long to be ready again. There was no way she'd be ready for another round though. Not without sustenance. "You hungry?"

Her entire face lit up as she nodded. All his muscles pulled tight as he watched her rinse the last soapy remains off her body. She stepped out onto the tile, just beyond the frosted glass enclosure and grabbed one of the fluffy towels. She wrapped herself in it but halted when he didn't follow suit.

"Aren't you coming with me?"

He nodded. "I just want to wash my hair and I'm sure you need to get dressed."

"Okay, I'll see you in a few."

She turned to leave but he stopped her. "Emma?"

"Hmm?"

"Don't wear any underwear today."

Her cheeks tinged pink as her lips tugged up at the corners. "We'll see."

* * *

Once in her room, Emma blow dried some of the dampness out of her hair but didn't feel like messing with the rest of it. She twisted her thick hair in a low chignon, swept on a layer of mascara and applied some lip gloss, not that she really needed it. As she studied herself in the mirror, it was hard to believe she was looking at the same person as three days ago. She looked...happy. And satisfied.

For most of her life, she'd erected tight, high walls around herself. She'd had to. Her "friends" back home wouldn't miss her. How could they miss someone they never even knew? Though Ricardo had sworn up and down she could sleep with whomever she wanted to, or carry on discreet liaisons, she'd never taken the risk. What if she'd fallen in love? Then what? Ricardo wouldn't have let her escape their deal. The stupid deal he forced her into by threatening her mother's life. That was the same reason she'd never had any real friends since college. It was a lonely existence but at least no one would get hurt or killed because of her. She couldn't live with that kind of guilt.

For the first time in her life, she wanted to let herself get close to someone. To let herself feel. Now, when she most positively couldn't. She glanced away from her reflection and retreated to the bedroom. She pulled on a pair of jeans, and slipped on a soft Victoria's Secret hooded sweatshirt. No bra either.

She started to head downstairs when the notebook on her desk caught her eye. Chewing her bottom lip, she picked it up. It was the number for the FBI Miami Division. According to her on-line research, all calls were anonymous. The bedside clock said it was only nine o'clock.

Quickly, she locked the bedroom door and picked up the phone before she could change her mind. She sighed in relief to hear a dial tone. Her hands shook as she dialed the number but she didn't hang up even though every fiber in her body screamed that she should.

On the third ring a woman with a pleasant, soothing voice picked up. "FBI, Miami Division. How can I help you?"

Emma opened her mouth to speak but no words would come.

"Hello?"

"Uh, yes, hello. I'd like to speak to Special Agent Sierra."

"He's not in. May I direct you to another agent?"

"No. When will he be in?"

"Monday morning but if this is an emergency, I can direct you to any one of our—"

"No thanks." She hung up the phone before the woman could protest further. She'd done a few searches of John Sierra and the man had won numerous achievement awards. He didn't seem like the kind of man to take bribes. Not that she could know anything for sure. Only time would tell.

Not much to go on, she knew but she couldn't hide any longer. The guilt was eating at her from the inside. Clawing at her mind and her heart with eagle talons. She'd had plenty of time to think things through. Too much in fact and now she couldn't hide anymore. She'd stay until Monday and enjoy every moment until then. She had a lot of memories to pack into a couple days but she was counting on those memories to keep her strong later when she was alone.

* * *

Caleb put on aftershave, something he hadn't done in over a year and dressed in jeans and a green cashmere sweater he'd probably worn twice since buying it.

He slipped his cell phone into his back pocket and went in search of Emma. Voices and laughter trailed down the hallway. An irrational swell of jealousy surged through him and by the time he reached the open doorway to the kitchen, he had to unclench his fists.

Emma stood at the stove with her back to him. Robert leaned against the counter on one elbow and was apparently saying something funny because she kept shaking her head and laughing. She wore snug fitting jeans that outlined her ass perfectly and he wanted more than anything to strip her down again and take her on the counter. And he also wanted to deck his best friend. His happily married best friend who was just being himself. She was seriously fucking with his head.

"Hey man, we were just talking about you." Robert finally noticed his presence.

"What about?" Even to his own ears, he sounded strangled and unnatural.

Emma glanced back at him, eyes filled with laughter and nodded. A half grin lit her face but she didn't say anything before turning back to the stove.

"What about?"

"You'll have to ask her. I just came by to see if you were going to be helping me out today. Most of the men are off and there are a few fences that need to be—"

"It can wait until Monday." His words were abrupt and he immediately regretted his tone.

Eyebrows raised, Robert pushed off from where he leaned against the counter, looked at Emma then at him and grinned. It wasn't an all-out smile that Emma would notice but he didn't miss the knowing gleam in his friend's eyes.

"Sure man. Izzy's been after me to put up some new shelves in the guest room anyway."

Seconds later, they were outside, walking through the garage toward the barn.

"That was fast work. Especially for you." Robert slapped him on the back.

Caleb knew what he meant but didn't take the bait. "What are you talking about?"

He rolled his eyes. "Don't even try that bullshit with me. You looked ready to pummel me for just talking to her. So either something happened already or you're pissed because—"

"All right man. Enough." It wasn't that Robert would breathe a word to any of the men if he told him but it was nobody's business what went on between him and Emma. The last thing he wanted to do was embarrass her.

"Hey, don't get me wrong. I'm happy for you. After that bitch Heather, you deserve to get laid. You just better not screw this up. She's the best cook we've ever had."

The tension in his chest eased and he shook his head. "Get out of here or I'll tell Izzy you like another woman's cooking better."

"All right, I can take a hint." He turned on his heel and headed toward his truck but he apparently couldn't resist a parting shot. "Maybe she's after you for your money."

His friend's laughter trailed behind him all the way to his vehicle.

Caleb shook his head and inwardly grinned. Robert and a few of the men knew his real monetary worth but it wasn't common knowledge that he was a millionaire several times over. During his twelve years away in the military, his father had made more than a few lucrative real estate investments. He was set for life, but in a few years he wouldn't need his father's money because he'd managed to do what his father never had.

He'd become one of the top breeders in the country. And it had only taken him five years to do it. Not that any of that mattered at the moment. The only thing he cared about was the sexy brunette in his kitchen.

He opened the door to the kitchen and silently watched as Emma darted around the room, preparing the rarely used, small table in the corner for them. He was glad she hadn't set them up in the dining room. She glanced up from setting out one of his mother's cloth napkins and smiled.

"I thought it would nice if we ate here instead. It's cozier."

"Do you need help with anything?"

She shook her head and a few tendrils of her silky hair escaped the tightly wound twist. "Nope. Just sit down and stay out of my way."

Even her bossiness turned him on. "Yes, ma'am." He pulled out a chair at the round table and hungrily watched her.

She moved with such grace and ease and when she reached up into one of the cupboards to grab two small plates, he got a nice view of her exposed back. He sucked in a deep breath, then inwardly cursed.

If a sneak peek of her back turned him on this much after they'd already made love, he was in serious trouble. And since when did he think of sex as making love? It took all his willpower not to move in behind her and nibble on the sensitive spot behind her ear.

"What are you cooking?" he asked mainly to distract his wayward thoughts.

She took the pan off the stove and walked over to him. "Southwestern omelets, bacon and grits."

"You know how to make grits? I'm impressed." He waited until she sat down to start eating.

"I told you I came from a large family."

She served herself almost as much as she'd served him. "And where exactly do you come from?"

She paused, fork in midair and her eyes locked on his. "Does it matter for now?"

He shrugged, mainly to cover the disappointment he felt that she wouldn't confide in him. "It would just be nice to know something about the very sexy woman I'm sleeping with."

He received a small smile, but just as quickly she frowned and chewed on her bottom lip. He could practically see the gear shifts turning in that pretty head of hers. Finally she sighed. "Caleb, I've got a lot of stuff I'm trying to figure out right now in my life and you're just another complication."

He started to protest but she cut him off. "A very good complication. And the last thing I want to do is be less than truthful with you, so if you ask me something and I can't answer, I'd rather not answer at all than lie. Does that work for you?"

He didn't have a choice did he? The last thing he wanted to do was scare her off. "I guess so. For now."

She nodded, then answered softly. "Thank you for being so understanding."

"Can I still ask questions? I know you might not answer but I'd like to know more about you other than you were a virgin until last night."

He got just the response he was expecting. Her face flamed at his words and she glared at him. "Fine. Go ahead. Ask away."

He chewed on another bite of the eggs, giving her a chance to gain back some of her composure before drilling her. "How is it that you were a virgin? You told me you broke off an engagement."

She chewed slowly and took a sip of her milk but wouldn't look him in the face.

"Emma?"

When she put her glass down, white liquid sloshed over the side but she didn't seem to notice. He could see another battle raging inside her. "He was gay."

He raised an eyebrow. "What?"

"I said he was gay. As in homosexual. Plain and simple. I've been his cover for years for reasons I am *not* going to get into and I finally had enough. It's stupid that he feels the need to hide something like that, but in his line of work, I guess . . . I just don't want to get into it. No more questions. Please? I don't have the energy this morning."

The pleading note in her voice nearly undid him. And he was fairly certain she was telling the truth. "Okay."

So, she'd left a man because he was gay? He could deal with that. It still didn't explain why she was on the run. He'd seen real fear in her eyes the first day they'd met. Had someone threatened her?

"So do you think you might show me some of your land?" Her voice brought him back to reality. She looked at him expectantly and some of the brightness had returned to her eyes.

"Definitely. We can go now if you're ready." Both of their plates were nearly clean and if they didn't leave this very instant, he was likely to strip her down and fuck her on the kitchen table. When she nodded, he picked up the dishes and put everything in the sink. "We can deal with this stuff later."

"Okay but..." She shifted from one foot to the other.

"But what?"

Her cheeks tinged pink. "Well, I'm not wearing a bra and it's a little cold out there."

He grinned and pulled her tight against him. Her breasts flattened against his chest and he dropped a kiss on her forehead. He ran his hands up underneath the back of her sweater, savoring the feel of her smooth skin under his touch. When she arched closer to him, he almost changed his mind about showing her around. "I'm glad you listened," he murmured into her thick hair.

"I didn't think I had much of a choice." She pulled her head back and searched out his lips with her own. It wasn't exactly chaste but it wasn't hot and passionate either. It was a sweet kiss. Sweet and unexpected.

She stepped out of his embrace and pivoted on her heel before he could protest. A few minutes later, she was back and had brought an extra sweater with her.

She grabbed his hand with her smaller one and linked fingers before pulling him toward the door. "Ready?"

He nodded, unused to the strangely intimate gesture. He'd never held hands with anyone before. None of his relationships had ever progressed that far. Now that he thought about it, he realized he'd never even held hands with his ex. It was something so simple. Something couples in love did. *Love?* Where had that thought come from.

He shook his head at his own absurd thoughts and locked the door behind them with his free hand. Their boots crunched over the fallen leaves as they crossed his yard in silence. He wasn't a big talker and it didn't seem she was either. If she didn't have something to say, she didn't try to break the silence with meaningless words. He stole a few glances at her and couldn't get over the excitement playing across her face. Excitement and wonder and something else he couldn't pin down. Regret? It didn't fit in with her bright eyes but the way she kept chewing on her bottom lip had him worried.

"You okay over there?"

She looked up at him and the raw appreciation in her shining dark eyes nearly pierced his heart. "Of course I'm okay. It's just so beautiful around here. All this land and no traffic or city noises. I can't get over how peaceful it is. I'll be honest, I've never spent much time in the country but now I understand why people choose to move away from the city. It's like a little slice of heaven."

His heart swelled a little but he understood exactly what she meant. The land they were on had been in his family for generations. To hear her talk about it with such awe touched a deep place in his heart. A place he'd forgotten existed.

A few white clouds dotted the pale sky and lush, green countryside surrounded them for miles. The glassy pond behind his house glistened under the new sun as docile ducks and swans soaked up the rays. With the exception of the whinnying horses, the world was silent and peaceful. Sometimes he got so caught up in work, he forgot to appreciate where he lived.

CHAPTER NINE

After saddling up the horses and finally coaxing Emma to get on one, they started off across the field toward a favorite spot of his. Oak and pine trees rustled around them as they trotted along one of the well-worn trails. It had been so long since he'd ridden for pleasure. Hell, it had been years since he'd taken a Saturday for himself. He worked damn near seven days a week.

"Where exactly are you taking me and how long until we get there?" Emma's panicky voice broke into the calm of the morning ride.

He glanced over and chuckled. She clutched the saddle horn with both hands so tightly he could see the whites of her knuckles. He'd given her his tamest horse, Peanut, and rigged the old mare with the softest, most comfortable saddle he owned.

"I thought you were excited about this."

"I was . . . I am. I just didn't realize how far up from the ground I'd be," she said through gritted teeth.

"Are you telling me you've never been on any kind of horse? Not even a little Shetland at a child's birthday party or something?"

She snorted in a very un-Emma like manner. "No. My father would have deemed riding horses a useless activity. I used to think he was such a snob but now I'm having second thoughts."

"Relax your body. You're too tense. Just pretend you're riding me."

Her head whipped up and she stared at him, her cheeks tinging that sexy pink again, but at least it worked. She loosened her grip on the horn and wasn't holding on for her life anymore.

"You tricked me," she grumbled after a while of riding in silence.

"It worked."

Finally she grinned, although he did notice that she kept glancing down at Peanut as if she were afraid he'd bolt at any moment.

"I didn't think you were the type of girl to be afraid of anything."

"Hey, you try shopping at Aventura Mall on Black Friday, then we'll talk about being afraid. I'm a lot tougher than I look." She flexed her non-existent arm muscle, her expression relaxed and he felt as if he was seeing the real her.

Aventura Mall? She was slipping. Letting little facts about her other life slip through. Good. That meant she was getting more comfortable with him. "I don't go to malls. Ever."

She shook her head good-naturedly and rolled her eyes heavenward. "Why am I not surprised? I bet you shop at Cowboys-R-Us."

A low, unfamiliar rumble erupted from his chest and it nearly sucked the life out of him a minute later when he realized what was happening to him. He was falling in love with her. If he wasn't there already. He'd never felt this way about another woman. Nothing even remotely similar. This comfortable camaraderie. Not only was she gorgeous and smart, he genuinely liked her company. Maybe it wasn't love, but he was headed there. When he'd kicked his ex out he hadn't felt an ounce of regret.

"What's got you looking so serious all of a sudden? Oh hell, are you lost?" Her lips quirked up, revealing a tiny dimple that only added to her innocent appearance.

He shook his head and his thoughts away. "We're here."

"We are?" She glanced around, looking confused and a little disappointed.

"Almost." He dismounted from his horse, then reached up to help her down.

He linked his hands under her arms and when her body slid down against his, he fought his already raging hard-on. Even after being on a horse for over an hour, she still smelled amazing. He wrapped his arms around her and inhaled the sweet smell of jasmine.

Her breasts flattened against his chest and he involuntarily surged his hips up against her body. His dick had a mind of its own. Whenever it got within a few feet of her, it had one goal and one goal only.

"You really didn't want to show me anything did you? You just wanted to get me out here all alone so you could do whatever you wanted to me?" She murmured against his neck before she teasingly nipped him with her teeth. Her voice had taken on a husky, sensuous quality and there was no denying she'd probably let him do whatever he wanted. All he had to do was ask.

With inhuman strength, he pulled himself away from her lean body, grabbed his pack down from the horse and tugged on her hand when all he really wanted to do was tug that tight little sweater right over her head. "No, although that doesn't sound like such a bad idea. Come on."

"What about the horses?" She glanced behind them, apparently unaware of how hot she was making him.

"They'll be fine. We'll walk from here." He'd looped their reins over a large tree branch. Not sturdy but his horses were trained.

"What's in there?" she asked, motioning to the backpack he now wore.

Shrugging, he held her hand in his and for the second time that day. The dirt path in front of them narrowed but it was still big enough for the two of them.

Just not wide enough for two horses. After ten minutes of walking, the path ended and opened up into an oasis.

Caleb kept his eyes trained on Emma, gauging her expression. He wanted her to love his place as much as he did. Needed her to.

Her eyes widened when they stepped through the clearing of trees and without taking his eyes off her, he knew what she was seeing. Her grip on his hand tightened.

Tall oak and palm trees shaded the private natural spring he'd never shared with anyone. The pool of aquamarine water glistened like the Caribbean ocean. The water was seventy-two degrees year round, though she wouldn't know that. It was his own small slice of paradise. Right after high school he'd joined the Marines when he was barely eighteen. Twelve years was enough though, so five years ago, right after his thirtieth birthday, he'd retired and taken over his father's horse farm. After spending over a decade as a sniper and going months at a time without talking to another human being, coming back to civilization, even somewhere as small as Lake City, had been an adjustment at times. So, he used the secret place of his childhood when he needed space.

"Wow." She expelled a long breath, as if she'd been holding it in.

"I'm glad it was worth your hideous horse ride." He leaned down and planted a kiss on her cheek.

She turned and smiled at him. "Now do I get to see what's in your backpack?"

"Yes." They walked to the water's edge where he knelt on the ground and pulled out an oversized quilt. Then he pulled out a small cooler with two wine glasses and a container with a mix of champagne and orange juice.

"Is that mimosas?" Her dark eyebrows lifted in surprise.

"Yeah, why?"

"Nothing, I'm just surprised. I guess I didn't peg you for a champagne kind of guy."

"There's a lot you don't know about me. Just as there's a lot I don't know about you." He glanced up from what he was doing and lifted his eyebrows.

Her jaw twitched but she didn't take the bait. Instead, she sat down on the quilt and took one of the glasses from him. "It might be early but after that ride, I think a little alcohol is in order."

"Agreed." He poured both glasses halfway and stretched out next to her.

She placed her glass on a solid patch of grass and leaned back on her elbows. "So what's the plan for today?"

He shrugged "No plan."

She grinned at him in what he could only describe as a mischievous manner. "Good, then we can take advantage of being alone out here."

"I like that look in your eyes."

Without responding, she sat up, rolled over and straddled him. She grabbed his arms and locked them over his head. It wasn't as if he couldn't move if he really wanted to but surprisingly, the feel of her holding him down turned him on more than he imagined.

"You're not too sore?" he rasped out.

She shook her head and ran her tongue over her lips. He swallowed hard when she positioned herself a little farther down and undid the front of his pants. He rarely wore boxers and today was no different. As she pushed his jeans over his hips, her intent expression heated up.

His balls tightened almost painfully when she bent over him. Still straddling him, her dark hair pillowed down around them both. When she tentatively licked his hard length, his hips bucked slightly at the soft, unexpected touch. He understood what she was doing. Something told him she'd never done this before and wanted to explore every inch of him. Not that he minded. She could lick, bite and touch him wherever and whenever she chose.

She licked and feathered kisses along his shaft before taking the head of him in her mouth.

"Oh shit," he groaned.

Wide eyed, she abruptly sat up from what she was doing. "Is it not..."

"Don't even finish that thought." Everything she was doing felt so good he was afraid he wouldn't last longer than a minute.

He pulled a condom from his back pocket before kicking off his jeans and practically ripping off his sweater. Kneeling on the quilt, she no longer straddled him but instead looked up at him with a hungry expression on her face.

"It's been too long since I've seen you naked."

She clutched the bottom of her sweater. "Here?"

He rolled the condom on, but only nodded because he didn't trust his voice. She stared at him and he could see those gears turning in her head again. She was searching for something in his eyes and he hoped she found it.

When her arms fell to her sides, he knelt in front of her. Instead of stripping her though, he touched his mouth to her soft lips and eased them apart. She might be ready to explore his body and she definitely wanted him but it was apparent she had reservations about being naked out in the open.

Never in a million years could Emma have imagined she'd be making love to someone outdoors. She'd never thought of herself as the adventurous type but as soon as Caleb had pulled out mimosas for them, she'd been lost.

Mimosas of all things! He looked so tough and a little intimidating but he'd been nothing but gentle and sweet with her. For the first time in her life, she knew what it might be like to love someone else. Not that she loved him. No way. She couldn't afford that. Not now. Maybe never.

It should have felt strange with him completely naked and her fully clothed but it didn't. If anything, it put her at an advantage. She raked her hands and fingers along his muscular chest and down his stomach, taking pleasure when he sucked in a ragged breath. His entire body was rock hard, yet he trembled.

Something told her that he rarely, if ever, shook and it empowered her that she got such a tangible reaction out of him. With both of her hands, she grasped his erection and in slow, smooth strokes, ran her hands up and down his shaft. Just as she'd done with her tongue.

He let out a feral growl and tugged her sweater over her head. Her exposed nipples hardened even more under the cool air and heat pooled between her legs, partly because of the erotic situation but mainly because of the way he stared at her.

Pure male appreciation pulsed out of his every pore. Caleb roughly gripped her hips, flipped her on her back and straddled her. He unzipped and pulled her pants completely off, his eyes darkening. "You're not wearing..."

She bit her bottom lip and shook her head. "You told me not to," she whispered.

Open to the cool air and his intense gaze, her nipples tingled almost painfully. She felt so exposed because of her state of undress. Being spread-eagle on a quilt in the middle of the woods didn't help either. His fingers skimmed along her stomach, sending shivers throughout her body, then one of his hands strayed between her legs. He teased and rubbed her clit for a brief moment before his hands returned to her hips.

His grip on her was tight, almost uncomfortably so, and he stared down at her with blazing, guarded eyes. She knew he wanted her, that much was obvious. But something else lingered in the endless depths and she wished more than anything she knew what he was thinking.

"Where have you been all my life?" he murmured before thrusting inside her.

He hadn't even tried to prime her with his fingers or mouth. She didn't need it. Wet and slick, her body accepted him without protest. Ached for him. Her inner walls were already making rapid contractions, clenching around him tighter. She moaned deep in her throat and wrapped her legs around him. His mouth found hers and she let out another moan as his raw, masculine scent overwhelmed her. Involuntarily, she arched her back, taking him deeper.

That only seemed to incite his desire more. She clawed his back the harder he pushed and held back a sob at the ecstasy flooding her veins. She'd never imagined such binding emotions were possible between a man and a woman. Now she understood completely why other women were so protective of their significant others. The knowledge that she'd be leaving soon burned a hole inside her but she pushed it away. Caleb was hers in the here and now. She couldn't dwell on the future.

With a final thrust, he found his release. Her body racked and shuddered right along with his. Afterward, he lay on top of her, both of them gasping for breath. When more than a few minutes had passed, she giggled and nudged him with her hand.

He groaned and rolled off her but took her hand in his large one. The gesture was so sweet, so intimate, she wanted to weep knowing she had to leave soon.

"I'm never going to get any work done with you around now," he grunted.

She smiled and started to comment, then stopped herself. She'd be leaving in a couple days. He might not know that but she did and she couldn't joke casually about their future when she knew it would be a lie. She couldn't do that to him. Not to Caleb.

Instead, she rolled closer to him. He wrapped his arm around her shoulders and she laid her head on his chest.

His staccato heartbeat took several minutes to even out and by the time it did, she was already drifting off.

"Tired," she managed to mumble. A vague awareness of his hand stroking her back in a gentle rhythm registered and she heard him say something but her brain couldn't comprehend his words.

* * *

Emma opened her eyes and fought off the cobwebs and confusion. A grayish blue sky loomed above her and it took a moment to register that it must be getting late. She was still naked but Caleb must have pulled the quilt around her. Fighting the panic in her throat, she sat up and scanned the woods for any sign of life. Before she saw him, she heard him crunching over the foliage behind her.

She half turned and smiled. A sudden shyness threatened to overwhelm her and she wasn't sure why. Maybe it had something to do with him being completely clothed.

"We need to get going before the sun sets."

How had it gotten so late? Crickets chirped noisily and a sharp breeze blew up, rustling the trees and cooling her body. She nodded and scrambled around for her clothes, ignoring his heat-seeking gaze. "How long have you been awake?" she asked, mainly to break the silence as she dressed.

"A couple of hours." His answer was simple but she was under the impression that something had happened while she'd been asleep.

She couldn't put her finger on it but something about him was different. What could have happened though?

"Is everything okay?" she asked as she zipped up her boots and pulled her jeans down over them.

"Yep." He nodded and packed up the quilt and the rest of their things.

In silence, she followed him out of the clearing and watched as he packed up the horses. Next, he helped her up onto hers and led them down the same trail they rode in. Other than the normal woodsy sounds and the clopping of the horses, their breathing was the only thing breaking the still atmosphere. Normally she didn't mind the quiet but this was the loudest silence she'd ever experienced.

"So this is your family's land?"

His head whipped around in surprise, as if he had forgotten her presence but at least he answered. "Yes."

When a few more minutes in silence passed, her patience nearly ended. "Caleb!"

"What?" He frowned at her.

"What's going on? Ever since I woke up you've said two words to me and that's only because I had to drag them out of you. Do you regret what happened between us because I'm a big girl—"

"No!" The abruptness of his answer calmed her nerves a little but it still didn't give her an answer to his strange behavior.

"Then what's up?"

"I want to talk to you tonight, after dinner and I've just been trying to figure out how to bring it up."

The knot in her stomach tightened and she could barely swallow the lump in her throat. Either he knew who she was or he wanted to end things. "That sounds ominous."

His piercing green eyes held hers in a steady gaze. "It's not."

"Okay."

The rest of the ride was silent but it wasn't uncomfortable. Once they were back at the stables, he took care of the horses.

"Don't you need help with anything?"

He half smiled and shook his head. "No. I'll be inside in a little while if you want to shower. I need to shower too, then we'll have dinner."

"And talk?"

He nodded but at least his eyes had that familiar gleam of desire back. "Talk and then make love the rest of the night."

The rest of the night? Yeah, she could do that. She bit her lip to keep from grinning like a love sick fool.

CHAPTER TEN

Caleb whistled to himself as he ran a towel over his damp hair. He loved Emma. It was too soon and he didn't know shit about her but he knew he loved her. The thought seemed ridiculous, even to himself, but he did. He'd known it today by the spring.

A foreign feeling had settled in his gut the past couple days and being so new, it had taken him too long to realize he was happy. He liked his quiet life, especially after serving in some of the worst shit holes the world had to offer. Five years ago, he retired and had so far been satisfied with his life. Satisfaction and contentment were different from the new emotion he was experiencing. Without meaning to, Emma had railroaded her way into his life and his heart.

He flipped on his flat screen television and pulled on a pair of boxers. Out of the corner of his eye, shapes and blurs danced on the screen. Just when he was about to turn it off, an attractive face flashed across the screen. A very attractive, very familiar face.

Instantly alert, he turned up the volume. He couldn't believe what he was hearing. Or seeing. *International playboy questioned on charges of murder. Two young women were found dumped behind a Miami hot spot with their throats slit. The badly beaten women were last seen in the company of Ricardo Mendez and some of his known associates. His lawyer is denying all allegations. This isn't the first time he's been questioned by the police but this is the first time his girlfriend Emma Garcia has not been by his side. As many know, she is the daughter of the late infamous arms dealer, Javier Garcia, though she is perhaps better known for her philanthropic work with the homeless community and troubled teens...*

Caleb turned down the volume but continued to gaze at the screen. A picture of Emma Garcia smiled back at him. Though the woman had platinum blonde hair, wore a slim fitting black evening gown and was showing off jewelry that probably cost more than his new pickup truck, it was Emma Cole. No doubt about it. He might not have realized it was her if he hadn't spent the past few days inside her, memorizing every inch of her.

Emma looked better as a brunette, more natural. Dressed as she was in that picture she literally looked like a million bucks but he preferred her current look. Hell, who was he kidding? He wouldn't care if she had black and purple, short spiky hair. He wanted her any way he could get her.

Not that he should even be thinking of that. No, he should be worrying why the very pretty daughter of a deceased arms dealer was in his home. Before he could change his mind, he went to his office.

After what felt like an eternity, his laptop flared to life. He looked up one of the few people he knew would help him without asking too many questions. Pulling out his cell phone, he dialed an old friend of his from the service. He just hoped the number was still good.

Caleb hated to waste a favor for this but he didn't have a choice. Emma wasn't dangerous, of that he was certain, but she was scared. Though he didn't have a clue what was going on, he'd somehow figure this out. He had to. If she needed help, he was going to be the one to give it.

"Hello?" His friend picked up on the second ring.

"Hey Nick, its Caleb Ryder, how are you?"

Nick Daley's loud Boston accent hadn't changed a bit. "Shit man! How long has it been? Four, five..."

"Five years," Caleb said, grinning to himself. He'd fought alongside Nick in the desert and a couple other places that weren't on their official records.

"Either you're in jail or you're getting married. Which is it?"

Caleb snorted. "Neither but I do need a favor."

It should have felt strange that he hadn't talked to him in five years and was calling him for a favor but it didn't. There were very few people in his life he called friends but Nick was one of those rare ones he could call up in the middle of the night and ask to help hide a body, no questions asked.

"Shoot."

"You still got friends in high places?"

His friend snorted. "Always. I'm working for an international security outfit located out of Saint Augustine but I've still got a few contacts in the DEA and the FBI. And if you're really in trouble, I've got a friend with the CIA. Depends on what you need."

"Good. I need any information you can get on a woman named Emma Garcia, including all known associates. Last known address is somewhere in Miami."

"Are you talking about the daughter of Javier Garcia? I've seen her picture flashed on the news all week."

Was he the only person who'd never heard of either one of them until now? "Yeah, the one and only. Is that going to be a problem? I don't want you taking any heat for this."

"No, I just wanted to make sure we were on the same page. I'm assuming you don't want anyone knowing that you're asking about her?"

Caleb sighed and rubbed a hand over his unshaven face. He knew what could happen if his friend started asking questions to the wrong people and he didn't want those people sniffing around here, especially when he didn't know how much trouble Emma was in. If she was even in trouble at all. "You assumed right. If you can get this for me without any hassle, consider us even."

Nick was silent on the other end for a long moment. Then, in true Nick form he said, "Man, shut the fuck up. This doesn't make us close to even. Maybe if I pull you out of a burning building and name my firstborn after you we'll be halfway there."

Caleb shook his head even though his friend couldn't see him. He might have saved Nick's ass more than once but Nick had kept him laughing nonstop the last six years he'd been in the Marines. If anything, he owed him his sanity. Any man who could find humor in a sticky, triple canopy jungle filled with mutant bugs and armed drug runners tracking them with the sole intent to torture and kill, should get a freaking medal. "I've missed you man."

"Good, maybe you won't be such a stranger from now on. It's getting late but I'll get back to you in a couple of days, maybe a week but probably sooner. Is there a reason I should put a rush on this?"

How could he answer that? "Don't kill yourself, but this is important."

"Just tell me one thing. Please tell me you aren't fucking her."

He gripped the phone tighter but didn't answer. He couldn't afford to piss off the only person who could help him. "Call me when you've got something."

Once they disconnected, he pulled up a search engine on his computer and searched Emma Garcia. Photos and articles covering various social events immediately popped up. In almost every picture, she was linked with the same man. Infamous arms dealer Ricardo Mendez.

* * *

Emma wiped off the foggy mirror and stared at her reflection. She almost didn't recognize herself. It wasn't the slightly altered appearance, because she'd gotten used to her natural hair color by now. No, it was everything about her. Her skin and eyes practically glowed. She looked like she'd spent a weekend at a full service spa. And it was all thanks to the rugged cowboy downstairs. How had this happened? How had he gotten under her skin so quickly?

In a couple of days, she'd be gone. And in a few weeks, he'd probably forget about her anyway. He didn't seem like the kind of man who depended on anybody. Sure, he asked a lot of questions about her past but he never opened up about himself. It's not as if she'd actually asked him but he seemed so closed off and private, she didn't see the point. No use getting even more attached than she already was.

After a quick glance at the clock, she finished towel drying her hair and dressed in a simple V-neck cashmere sweater and black pants. She figured Caleb would be done with his shower by now. Her feet were silent as she descended the wooden stairs.

When she found his room empty, she tried his office. As a courtesy, she started to knock on the partially open door when she heard Caleb say her name.

Her real name.

Hand still raised, she froze in place and listened. The words were muffled and slightly jumbled but she knew what she heard.

"Emma Garcia…identity…find out what you can…"

Bile rose in her throat and she resisted the urge to storm into his room. Is this what he wanted to talk to her about? Without making a sound, she retreated to her room. She laced up her sneakers, grabbed her keys off the dresser and threw her dirty clothes into one of her bags. After zipping it up, she heaved one bag on her shoulder and took the other one in her hand. Luckily, she hadn't unpacked most of her stuff. She eased open the door to her room and listened.

Before she could chicken out, she quietly but quickly raced down the stairs, through the long hallway and out the kitchen door. She cringed when she realized the garage door was closed. Without wasting another second debating the noise it would make, she punched the button and sprinted across the yard. Carrying two bags slowed her down but she couldn't afford to leave any of her stuff behind.

An eerie calm permeated the night air. Her sneakers crunched over leaves and fallen branches and she could see her breath in front of her. Her entire body shook with barely controlled tremors but it wasn't from the cold. Adrenaline and fear ripped through every vein and nerve ending in her body.

She couldn't believe Caleb knew who she was. Had he been planning to turn her in? She'd been so close to trusting him, to confessing everything. None of that mattered now. She needed to get as far away from him as possible. She'd find a cheap motel somewhere and decide what to do in the morning. Sleep would be impossible but at least she'd be safe.

Clutching her side, she tried to ignore the cramp taking over the left side of her body. Except for a couple of horses that whinnied in the distance, there were no sounds or obstacles in her way. According to Caleb, most of the men had houses scattered across his land but none lived too close to him.

She jiggled the door to the shack where her truck was housed and exhaled a breath she hadn't realized she'd been holding. It creaked and groaned as it swung open but by now, she didn't care how much noise she made. She was almost free. The key slipped into the ignition and she said a silent prayer that the vehicle started.

It coughed and sputtered but it turned over. She didn't know how that was even possible but it did. It kicked into drive, spitting up grass and gravel as she tore out of the dilapidated structure. Now it really didn't matter if anyone heard her. Cows or not, she was gone. But, as a small precaution, she kept the driving lights off. The dips along the dirt road were difficult to gauge but it wasn't long until she passed the house and realized the front gate was closed.

After a quick glance over her shoulder, she hopped out of the dying vehicle and unlatched the heavy chain. The metal door swung open easily and clanged against the connecting fence. A couple of cows mooed at her but she ignored them. She turned back but jerked to a halt at the sight in front of her. The only sounds reverberating in her head was her own breathing and the pounding of her heart.

In bare feet and boxers, Caleb stood in front of her, hands balled into fists, looking like a warrior. An angry warrior. The moon, about a billion stars and light from the main house illuminated him enough so that she could see his expression. She swallowed hard and took an involuntary step back, which only seemed to anger him more.

He advanced on her before she even had a chance to speak. Somehow, he crossed the nearly twenty foot distance between them in seconds. But, he didn't touch her. He just stared at her with his piercing green eyes, gluing her to the spot.

CHAPTER ELEVEN

"What. The. Fuck. Are. You. Doing?" Each word came out clipped, as if talking was a struggle for him.

"Leaving?" The word came out as a scratchy whisper and sounded more like a question than an answer. Like she needed his permission or something.

His jaw twitched uncontrollably and some indefinable emotion crossed his hardened face. "Get in the house."

"What?"

"Now. Walk or I'll carry you." He turned away from her and retreated to the truck.

She watched as he leaned in and ripped out the keys, then grabbed both her bags from the backseat. He slammed the door with such jarring force she jumped. He didn't wait for her, but stalked toward the house.

A shiver ran down her spine as she watched him walk away. Every sinewy muscle in his body was pulled taught. Unsure what he was going to do, she decided to follow. She had nothing to lose at this point. She couldn't outrun him and if he wanted to turn her in to the cops, so be it. That's what she'd been planning to do anyway. Eventually. She just hadn't imagined he would betray her.

When she made it to the entrance of the garage, she flinched. Caleb stood by the open door leading to the kitchen, waiting. In the harsh overhead light, his features were positively feral. His jaw was clenched tightly and despite her desire to stand strong against him, she looked down at her feet and walked into the kitchen. The sounds of the garage door shutting behind her echoed loudly in the quiet house.

"Stay here," he ordered, then disappeared with her bags in hand.

Five minutes later he returned wearing a long-sleeved T-shirt and sweatpants. She opened her mouth to speak but her jaw snapped shut when he shook his head. He turned toward the entry and nodded, as if she should follow him. She followed him down the hallway and into the living room. He took a seat on the long coffee-colored couch and she sat on the edge of the matching love seat.

When he still didn't say anything, she turned and stared out the open window that spanned most of the room. A small creek glistened under the moon but the only thing that really registered for her was the sound of their breathing.

Somehow she found her voice but still couldn't look at him. "I heard you on the phone. You know who I am. So, are the police on the way?"

"Did you happen to stick around for the whole conversation?" he ground out. The barely controlled anger in his words forced her to look at him.

Was this some kind of trick question? She knew exactly what she'd heard. "I heard you say my name. My real name. Pardon me if I didn't wait around. I trusted you." Her voice cracked a little but some of her earlier anger returned in the process, giving her needed courage.

She glared at him and crossed her arms over her chest. Trust wasn't something she gave out freely. When she'd heard him on the phone, she hadn't thought anything through. No, she'd reacted and done what came naturally. She ran.

He raked a hand through his damp, rumpled hair and sighed. "I saw a picture of you on the news. You look a lot different with that hair but I knew it was you. And I wasn't planning to turn you over to the police. I was trying to help you. I don't know why you ran but after Googling you, I know enough about that scumbag ex-boyfriend of yours to know that you had a good reason. What you heard, or what you think you heard is wrong. I was trying to see if I could help you."

His words pierced a hidden part of her heart. The part she kept locked away from the world. He knew who she was and wanted to help her? She sucked in a deep breath but couldn't stop the tears from streaming down her face. She never cried. Not even when her mother died. She swiped at the wetness and in the few seconds it took her to blink away her tears, Caleb was beside her.

A lump settled in her throat and she knew if she attempted to talk, the dam would break. He must have sensed her need to gain composure because he continued. "I called a buddy of mine when I recognized your face on the news. I asked him to get as much information on you as possible but not to make any waves."

She swallowed the baseball sized lump. If she couldn't trust Caleb, then she might as well turn herself over to Ricardo. "When I was eighteen my father died. And if you know who I am, then you must know who he was."

She was grateful when he nodded. Explaining her father would take more energy than she had.

"After his funeral I was looking for some privacy and stumbled upon Ricardo and someone...a man...well, you get the idea. Anyway, he shoved me up against the wall and threatened me with the thousands of ways he would kill me if I ever told anyone. As if I cared that he was gay. It's not a big deal but..."

Caleb took both of her hands in his and held them tightly. Knowing that he knew all about her and wasn't judging, gave her an inner strength. "The next day he showed up on my doorstep with flowers and asked my mother if he could court me. Court me! He actually used that freaking term." She rolled her eyes as she remembered that day.

"My mother is very traditional so he knew what would work on her. When he got me alone, he told me that he would kill her if I didn't play his stupid charade. In college, he occasionally checked in but he pretty much let me do my own thing. I was always too terrified to get involved with anyone though. What if I fell in love? Then what? Ricardo would never let me go. And it would have given him more leverage against me, more people to threaten." She moved closer into Caleb's embrace and leaned her head on his shoulder.

"Why did you finally leave?" he murmured against her hair.

"I saw something I shouldn't have." She clenched her teeth and her grip on his hands tightened. Visions assaulted her in waves and she had to fight the nausea that came on every time she thought about it.

He pried his hands from hers and wrapped both arms around her, pulling her practically into his lap. "Tell me what you saw Emma."

"I was looking for a favorite pair of earrings I wanted to wear. When I couldn't find them in my room, I went to the pool house. We have a heated indoor pool that I sometimes used for laps. Anyway, I heard yelling and noises the closer I got. Instead of turning around, I was stupid and decided to see what was going on."

She lifted her head back because she needed to see his face when she told him. "Ricardo and two of his bodyguards were standing over two women. Blood was everywhere. Matted in their hair, on the floor. I think they'd been dead a little while but I can't know for sure. All three men were yelling in unison but I couldn't hear anything over the sound of my own heartbeat. I got out of there before..."

Several minutes passed but finally he spoke. "You don't have to go on honey. I think I get the picture."

She was tempted to stop talking but the words came out in a rush. He had to understand. "I ran. I did the only thing I could think of. My mom died a few months ago and I don't have any close friends. I didn't know what else to do. I needed distance and time to think. I wanted to go to the police, believe me, but I couldn't go to the Miami police. Ricardo has too much influence and I didn't want to risk it. I didn't even think of the FBI until after my first night here. I was planning on leaving Monday, then I heard you on the phone and I freaked out."

His entire body stiffened against hers and he held her away from him. "You were going to leave Monday?"

She nodded. No use lying to him now. Not when he knew everything else about her. "Possibly Tuesday."

"Why?"

"I have to go to the FBI and tell someone what I saw. I'm terrified of Ricardo but the guilt is killing me."

"But, why not leave sooner? Why bother staying at all?" His voice was hoarse and raw.

"I'm selfish. I wanted you for just a couple more days before I left." The room was dark and she was grateful for the dim lighting. Heat crept up her neck and cheeks at the admission.

The corded muscles in his neck tightened and his jaw twitched. His next words shocked her more than anything she could have imagined. "I love you Emma. That's what I wanted to talk to you about tonight."

Her throat constricted, making it impossible to swallow. Her father had been an infamous arms dealer, she was on the run from her psycho ex-sort-of-boyfriend and he loved her?

His words had barely registered when he continued. "When I heard the sound of the garage door and realized you'd left, the bottom of my entire world fell out. A sickness like I've never experienced..."

His voice slightly cracked and he pulled her onto his lap. "I'm not letting you go honey. We'll figure this thing out together. If you want to go to the FBI, then I'm going with you. The friend I contacted tonight can help us.

If not, we'll set you up with a new identity. Hell, I'll move if that's what it takes. I've got land all over the country. We can move to North Carolina if that's what you want."

He'd do that for her? "Caleb, I need to go to the FBI. If you can set it up I'd appreciate it but if not, I don't expect—"

He placed a gentle finger over her mouth. "We'll talk about it in the morning. Right now you need sleep."

She wanted to argue. It was still relatively early but the entire night's events crashed in on her. All that mattered was Caleb trusted her. Loved her even. For now, she was safe.

He stood and pulled her to her feet. When they came to his bedroom door, she planted a light kiss on his cheek. "I'll be right back. I just need to change."

Caleb just pulled her back against him when she started for the stairs. "Your clothes are in my room."

"What? Why?"

"Your bags, everything, is in here. From now on, you're staying in my room. We'll unpack it all tomorrow. Now, come on."

He didn't let go of her hand, even as they walked into his room. After undressing her, he pulled back the covers and tucked her in. His hard-on was visible through his thick sweat pants, yet he made no move to touch her in an intimate way.

"Aren't you getting in to bed?"

"In a little while. I need to make some calls tonight."

Without explaining, she understood what he meant. She might not like it but now that she knew he was on her side she could rest easier. "Okay."

* * *

After he was sure Emma was asleep, Caleb retreated to his office and called Nick back.

"Hey man, I'm glad you called. I've already got some information," Nick said before he'd gotten a hello out.

He inwardly sighed and ignored every primal instinct inside him that told him to pack Emma up and disappear. "Yeah, well so do I."

He relayed everything she'd told him, leaving out a few details.

Nick let out a low whistle. "So that's why she disappeared."

"Well, that's one of the reasons." He didn't see the need to get his friend more involved than necessary.

"All right, what do you want to do?"

"I need to set up a meeting with someone you trust. You personally. Make it clear that she is going to be under my protection. I don't care about protocol or jurisdictional bullshit. She'll meet with them, make a statement and she's willing to testify. Until the trial, she's with me. If they try to put her in WitSec, we'll disappear. Get it?"

"Perfectly clear buddy. Stay by your phone. I think I know who can help you."

True to his word, Nick called back less than half an hour later.

"Tell me you have good news."

"Well..."

"Well what? If they don't play by my rules, we're gone." Emma's safety wasn't up for debate.

"They're not happy about it but for now, they've agreed to meet and take her statement. If what she has to say is worth it, then she can stay with you but only on the condition that a couple of agents are there too. Hell, anything is better than a crappy safe house."

He strummed his fingers on his desk. "Fine. Who's in charge of this task force?"

"His name is John Sierra. Maybe you've heard of him."

"I've seen him on the news a couple times. You trust him?"

"Definitely. I wouldn't set you up with him if I didn't. He wants to meet tomorrow afternoon."

Caleb clenched the phone against his ear. It was soon but maybe that was better than dragging it out. "Okay."

After writing down all the details, he poured a double whiskey and downed it without tasting it. He understood Emma's need to testify but part of him wanted to just leave. He re-set the alarm took the pistol from his office and went to his room.

Before climbing into bed, he checked both his weapons and slipped the extra one into the drawer on his side of the bed. Keeping two guns at the ready might seem a little excessive but he didn't give a shit.

Her sweet fragrance enveloped him the moment he lifted the comforter and slipped in next to her. Not wanting to wake her, he stretched himself along the length of her silky body and wrapped his arm around her waist. In her sleep, she snuggled tighter against him and made seductive purring sounds.

And now he'd never get to sleep.

Eventually he managed to doze, but a couple hours later the sudden blast of his cell phone caused him to jerk awake. Next to him Emma stiffened almost immediately.

It was close to three thirty in the morning. Emma's face tensed, mirroring what he was thinking. A call at this time wasn't a good thing.

It was Nick. "Hey," he said quietly.

"Sorry to call so late but there have been some developments. I put in a call to John Sierra to set everything up. A few hours later, he was gunned down outside his office. He's in intensive care but it looks like he's going to make it."

"What does this mean for Emma?"

"Someone hacked the system and so far a big chunk of computer files have been compromised. There might be a mole but it's hard to tell right now if this was internal. It could have nothing to do with Emma but with everything going on right now, I had to warn you."

"I'll alert my men and their families."

"There's one more thing," Nick said, his voice grim.

The note is his voice made Caleb tense. "Mendez is missing. It could mean nothing but I doubt you want to leave anything to chance."

That was an understatement. "What do you mean, missing?"

"After everything that happened with Sierra, there was a cluster-fuck of miscommunication and somehow he evaded the guys watching him."

He resisted the urge to throw his phone against the wall. "How long ago was this?"

"About three to four hours, give or take. I just found out or I would have called sooner."

As soon as they disconnected, Emma pounced. "Was that your contact? What did he want?"

"Honey, give me a sec." He ignored the hurt look in her eyes. He needed to warn everyone on his land. If the house or land came under attack, he wanted his men ready to fight. Some of them were ex-military and the ones that weren't knew how to fire a gun.

He dialed Robert first and they split the list between them on who to call. Out of the corner of his eye, he watched Emma retreat to the bathroom. Seconds later, he heard the sound of running water. By the time he finished up with his last call, she sat on the bed, fully clothed, with her arms wrapped around her knees.

"I guess I don't need to explain too much huh?"

She shook her head. "Does he know where I am?"

"Honestly, I don't know. Just to be safe, we're leaving for a couple days until this mess is settled. If he has even a clue as to your location, I don't want him within one hundred miles."

She ran a hand through her rumpled hair and sighed. "Can you afford to leave? I don't want—"

Like he'd let her out of his sight. "Robert can handle everything. Trust me, this place will survive."

"Well, I'm pretty much still packed. When do you want to leave?"

He glanced at the face of his cell phone. Four o'clock. At least they would beat any traffic. "Now."

She nodded and half smiled but he could see the worry lines return to her face.

CHAPTER TWELVE

Twenty minutes later his bags were packed, along with a cooler of drinks and food so they wouldn't have to make any stops. Emma still hadn't spoken more than a couple of words but he was giving her time. He only hoped she would get some sleep once they got on the road. God knew she needed it.

After loading up the truck in the garage and packing Emma in the front seat, all the lights went out.

"Caleb?" he heard Emma whisper and didn't miss the panic in her voice.

"I'm right here honey," he murmured from where he stood by the doorway. "Don't move. I'm coming to get you."

His steps across the concrete floor were silent and calculated. Seconds later, he held her delicate hand in his. "Follow me and when I give you the signal, I want you to get low to the ground." He had experience maneuvering around in the dark but he doubted she did.

"Okay," she whispered, her grip tightening. His eyes adjusted to the darkness as they maneuvered toward the kitchen door.

"Take a step up," he whispered.

As soon as they moved from the garage and stepped onto the tile of the kitchen, he applied pressure to her hand and pulled her toward the floor. They belly-crawled to the dining room and crouched at the dimly lit entrance. Light streamed in from the windows, giving them some guidance. Though low to the ground, he could see the lights on in the barn, which meant the power going out wasn't a mistake.

The distant sound of breaking glass somewhere within the house caused Emma to jump but he put a finger to his lips signaling her silence. She nodded, giving him reassurance that she wouldn't freak out and give away their position. If it was Ricardo, and his gut told him it was, he probably had the house surrounded.

As quietly as humanly possible, he asked Emma, "How many men does he normally have with him?"

She held up four fingers in response.

Not great odds but not terrible either. Chances were Ricardo hadn't had much time to call in a lot of backup, especially if he was trying to leave Miami unnoticed. If only Caleb could get Emma to safety first. He gave her one of his weapons and an extra magazine. Her eyes widened but she took it without complaint.

Staying in the crouching position, they shimmied to the side door in the dining room. From outside, it was hidden from view because of bushes and an oversized fig tree. Not to mention, the sensory lights hadn't gone off once. Since the lights weren't connected to the main power, he was fairly certain no one was waiting to ambush them.

A loud thud, then two curses from somewhere in the house reverberated in the silence. He thought he heard steps coming down the hallway but couldn't be sure, so he made a choice. They couldn't stay in the house any longer. If it was just him, he'd go on the offensive but he couldn't take a chance with Emma's life.

He opened the door and said a silent prayer that his gut instinct didn't fail him. They both crawled out onto the grass and hugged the side of the house. The sensory lights pointed in the other direction, so they crawled behind a cluster of bushes shadowing the small corner of the house. With Emma in front of him, he kept his weapon trained on the door.

If he could just get her to the fence line, she could crawl to safety and he could take care of the men in his house. Without the proper night vision equipment or even extra magazines, he felt devoid of his battle gear. Five years had passed since he'd been in a combat situation but some things a man never forgot. If it became necessary, he would kill with his bare hands. Anything to keep her safe.

He crawled in front of her and scanned the fence line and nearby trees. He couldn't see anyone or even a slight giveaway of human movement. They were probably all in the house, expecting them to be unarmed and sleeping. He handed her his cell phone and spoke softly in her ear. "Listen carefully. I want you to sprint to the fence line, then belly-crawl the length of it to the edge of the woods." She was small enough that she would be completely hidden by the bottom plank if she stayed low. Thankfully, she nodded.

"Call Robert. Tell him to call the local police and the Feds."

"What about you?" she whispered.

He shook his head and ignored the incessant hammer of his heartbeat. "Just go."

She shook her head and opened her mouth to protest when a flash from the direction of the barn lit up the sky.

"Now," he shouted above the noise and shoved her in the opposite direction. This might be the only advantage he got.

Staccato gunfire erupted into the still night air. It wasn't as if they were firing at each other, so odds were the men who worked for Caleb had arrived. Most of them were ex-military or just plain southern boys who grew up hunting. He wasn't worried about them holding their own. He stayed in his position, still scanning the woods for signs of life, until he saw Emma safely disappear behind the fence. Just as he primed himself to head toward the barn, the side door flew open.

Two masked men barreled out with no apparent heed for their own safety. Before either man had a chance to notice him backed against the house, Caleb emptied a couple of rounds into them. They dropped like deflated balloons. Without moving his weapon from the protective position, he checked both of their pulses and took both of their guns before proceeding.

The night had grown eerily silent again, all gunfire having completely quieted. Dying flames danced on what was left of the barn roof. Horses whinnied in the distance and he saw a few by the fence line so he assumed Robert had managed to free them. His only concern however, was Emma's safety.

He started to move toward the woods when a familiar song rang out from the direction of the woods. Robert was seventy-five percent Native American and for as long as he could remember, had used bird calls as way of communication out in the woods during hunting trips. The familiar sound of the finch alerted him that something was off.

Before he had a chance to figure out a plan of attack, two figures emerged from the edge of the woods. One of them was Emma and she had a gun pressed against the base of her spine.

Every couple of steps the man behind her shoved her viciously in the direction of the barn. To her credit, she didn't make a sound or fight him, which meant she was thinking rationally. Caleb hunkered down and slowly but methodically crawled along the wet grass and earth, sticking to the shadows and trees as he followed them. Since Emma and the man he assumed was Ricardo were heading toward the barn, their backs were half turned to Caleb giving him even more cover than just the night. If he'd had a rifle, there would be no problem but he was still fifty yards away and with a pistol, in the dark, it was damn near impossible to take the shot. Not with Emma's life in the balance.

The only thing that gave him a small sliver of hope was the fact that Emma was still alive. Ricardo probably knew his men were dead and was using her as a hostage to escape. If not, she wouldn't be walking or breathing. That was the only advantage Caleb had. Ricardo needed her alive.

Years of training kicked in and on some deeper level, he knew his entire life had been building up to this moment. Emma was his other half and he would protect her. It was the law of the jungle, as old as time itself. She was his and he would kill for her.

* * *

Emma fought to stay calm. The gun pressed to the back of her spine wasn't helping but if she wanted to get out of this alive, she had to. She'd been in the middle of calling Robert when Ricardo had come out of nowhere. He'd literally tackled her and taken her gun and phone. She knew Caleb was close by, or at least she hoped he was. Either way, she wasn't going down without a fight. Ricardo had taken her off guard once, but that wasn't going to happen again. Now she just had to wait for an opportunity to present itself. If she could take him by surprise, she would have a fighting chance. He'd already taken so much from her, she wasn't letting him take anything else.

"Where are you taking me?" They were rushing toward the barn but she had no idea what his ultimate plan was.

"Shut the fuck up. You've caused me enough trouble already."

"Why did you kill those girls?"

He shoved her so hard she stumbled but at least she didn't lose her footing. To her surprise, he answered. "They were taking pictures with their cell phones."

So what? Before she could question him further, he continued. "Stupid bitches were taking pictures of me and Carrington. I told those idiots who work for me I didn't care if they brought whores back to the house but they always seem to bring the biggest morons."

Carrington? Why did that name sound familiar? She couldn't worry about that now. Keep him talking. It was the only thing that might work. "So what if they took pictures? Why didn't you just take their phones away?"

"I tried to," he growled. "The stupid bitches thought it was so fucking funny to play keep away with their phones."

"So you slit their throats?"

"After I beat the shit out of them."

Her stomach roiled. He spoke so matter-of-factly, as if taking two lives meant nothing. Which they didn't, at least not to him.

She caught a whiff of ash and smoke as they neared the barn. The flames on the barn were dying down and she saw one of his many cars half-hidden behind two trucks. None of his men were in sight, which meant Ricardo probably knew his men were down and he was using her as his hostage. At least she had that going for her. He'd most likely keep her alive until they were off the property. Then he'd dump her in some roadside ditch like a piece of garbage. Not that she planned to give him the chance. If she could stall him long enough, she might be able to make a run for it. She'd rather be wounded or killed trying to escape than being shot execution style.

Her only regret was that she'd never get to tell Caleb she loved him. It was crazy. She knew that. They'd only known each other a short time but every fiber in her being knew it was love. Life sure had a fucked up sense of humor.

Just as they reached the corner of the barn, Ricardo jerked to a halt and moved the gun away from her spine. All the hairs on the back of her neck stood up and for once in her life, she followed her instincts. She covered her head and dived into the dirt.

Two loud pops sounded above her and after what seemed an eternity, she risked rolling over and sat up. Ricardo lay on the ground behind her and half his head was blown off. She never had time to register the horrific carnage because Caleb stood a few yards away. He had a gun in one hand, looking like the warrior she'd originally taken him for, and he held out his other one for her.

CHAPTER THIRTEEN

Hours later, Emma pulled the blanket Caleb had given her tighter around her shoulders, trying to absorb the scene in front of her. She sat on the back of his tailgate in the open garage as men in uniforms, men in suits and some of Caleb's cowhands milled around, barely acknowledging her presence. His men were cleaning up after the explosion and trying to round up the horses and the men in uniforms were doing whatever it was they were paid to do. It was only a matter of time before the FBI agents started in with their questions.

By now, the sun peeked on the horizon and she was coming down from her adrenaline high. She still couldn't believe Ricardo was dead. Not that she was sorry. She almost felt guilty for her lack of remorse. Almost. The cold steel of his gun against her spine was something she wasn't likely to forget for a while to come. That or the hideous venom he'd spewed in her ear as he pushed her toward the barn.

On the gravel driveway about twenty feet in front of her, Caleb, his back turned to her, talked to two men in suits. Every few minutes he'd turn around and give her what he probably thought was a reassuring look. At this point, nothing could reassure her. Now that daylight loomed she could see the lines etched into the grooves of his face and the bags under his eyes.

After what felt like an eternity, Caleb and one of the men in suits finally came to talk to her.

"Emma, this is Special Agent Mathew Woods. He has a few questions for you." Caleb leaned against the tailgate and draped a protective arm around her shoulders.

Garnering strength from Caleb's presence, she shook hands with the tall blond man she guessed to be in his early forties and found herself returning his genuine smile. Maybe this wouldn't be as bad as she'd pumped herself up to believe.

"I know you've been through a lot ma'am but the sooner we get this over—"

"I'm ready to answer your questions."

He nodded and pulled out a notepad and pen. "Okay, I have an idea of some things thanks to Caleb but we need everything on the record. Let's start at the beginning. Why did you run from Miami?"

"I saw Ricardo and two of his men standing over the bodies of two dead girls inside the pool house. Part of me had always known what he did for a living but I don't think it ever sank in until that moment." A shiver ran down her spine at the vivid vision that seemed to play over and over in her head. Caleb must have understood because he gave her shoulders a squeeze.

"Did you know the two girls personally?"

"No, they weren't any of his regular girls if that's what you mean. That was the first time I'd ever seen them."

"Regular girls?"

She half shrugged. "I saw a lot of the same faces at some of his parties and at the house in general."

"What kind of parties?"

She risked a glance at Caleb. "Would you mind getting me some coffee?"

"Sure." His jaw clenched but at least he didn't argue.

As soon as the connecting door leading from the garage into the kitchen shut behind him, she turned back to Agent Woods. "I don't know what else to call them except sex and drug parties. He invited what I guess you would call clients over to the house and I can only assume he provided them with women and drugs. The women looked like prostitutes to me but I can't say for sure. There were never any violent happenings at the house, at least not that I know of and I was only at the house for two of them. And that wasn't by choice. Both times, I locked myself in my room until I could escape. If I knew he was having a party, I stayed at my mom's house for a couple days."

He held out two photographs for her to view and by that time Caleb had returned. "Do you recognize these women? They were found behind a restaurant in the downtown area."

Two sets of lifeless eyes stared out of hollow, sunken faces. They were the faces from her nightmares. "Yes. Those are the same two women from the house. I assume he moved their bodies. Did you find out their names?"

She took the steaming mug from Caleb and inhaled the rich hazelnut aroma. Agent Woods nodded and took the pictures back.

"Yes we did. Originally, we thought they were prostitutes but they were just a couple of pretty young girls who were part of the Miami night life. They ended up in the wrong place at the wrong time." His jaw twitched as he shook his head and slipped the pictures into his coat pocket.

"Ricardo told me they were taking pictures of him and someone named Carrington. The name sounds familiar but I still can't place it. Anyway, I guess things got out of hand and he killed them. He didn't elaborate if he had any help but obviously no one stopped him. Basically it sounded like the girls annoyed him, so he killed them."

The other man nodded but didn't comment further. He just jotted down more notes.

She gripped Caleb's hand with her free one and squeezed. "Is Caleb going to be in any trouble for what happened?"

Agent Woods' mouth curled up slightly at the corners. "I think I can safely say that this is a clear case of self-defense." He cleared his throat and shot Caleb a look she could only describe as uneasy.

What was going on? She'd answered his questions. She glanced back and forth between the two men. "Am I missing something here? Ricardo's dead. Am I in trouble for leaving?"

Caleb cleared his throat. "They want to search his house. Since you live there too, and—"

"Go ahead. You can do whatever you want as far as I'm concerned. I don't know the combination to either of his safes but I do know where he keeps the key to a safety deposit box. I don't know which bank it goes to but I'm sure you guys can figure it out. I also know..." She trailed off, unsure if she should go on. Ricardo had left a wake of violence in his life and death. How many more lives did she want involved?

"What is it hon?" Caleb's deep voice poured through her veins, soothing her.

She swallowed and cleared her throat, ignoring the small twinge of her conscience. "Well, I know where his boyfriend lives but I don't want to get him in any trouble because he's really sweet. Ricardo treated him the same way he treated everyone else, like garbage. I don't know why he stayed—"

"Boyfriend?" The agent's eyes widened a fraction.

"Uh, yeah, didn't Caleb tell you?"

Caleb shook his head. "I figured that was up to you to decide. I didn't know if you wanted that made public."

"I couldn't care less. I'd rather people know the real reason I stayed, instead of having them think I dated a monster of my own free will. If you can leave his boyfriend's name out of this though, I would appreciate it."

"I don't think that will be a problem. On another note, do you know any of his associates who would have something against you?"

She resisted the urge to laugh at the term associates. "Not that I know of. To be honest, I wouldn't recognize any of his so-called associates if I ran into them on the street. We rarely spent time together. I only went with him to big-name parties when he wanted to schmooze with legitimate people. It's not as if we took vacations together and he was rarely at the house. If he was, I usually wasn't."

Agent Woods flipped his notebook shut and tucked it into his jacket pocket. "I think we're about done here. If what you say is true, you were only a threat to him directly so you should be safe."

"Should be?"

"As safe as anyone can be. Trust me Ms. Garcia, we wouldn't be leaving you without protection if we thought you were in danger."

"You're leaving?"

"As soon as they finish up with the rest of the bodies, we'll be out of here. I assume you won't be leaving the country any time soon?"

"No, I'll be heading back to Miami as soon as possible. You know how to contact me if you need me."

He shook her hand and then Caleb's before disappearing into the house.

"You're leaving?"

She looked up in surprise at the defensive tone in Caleb's voice. "Well, yeah. There's a lot of stuff I need to take care of."

"I see." He removed his arm from her shoulder, his big body tense.

"What does that mean? You see?"

"Are you coming back?" he asked quietly.

"Did you think I was going to just leave and never see you again?"

He shrugged but she didn't miss the raw flash of fear in his gaze.

"If you think you can get rid of me that easily you're out of your mind." Too tired to move from her seat on the tailgate, she pulled him so that he stood in between her legs, wanting to reassure him. How could he even be worried about that?

His green eyes flared to life when she placed her hands on his chest. "Well, we never really talked about the future and..."

"I'll admit that it might take some getting used to living in such a small town but I've wanted to leave Miami for as long as I can remember. I don't have any real friends because I couldn't risk caring about anyone. The reason I'm going home is to pack up my stuff, put the house on the market, say goodbye to everyone I worked with at the homeless shelter and get all my mother's stuff out of storage."

"The house is in both your names?"

She shook her head. "No, but I'm his sole beneficiary."

Caleb's eyebrows rose but when he didn't comment, she continued, "I know it's weird, but I've seen his will before. I'm not sure why he wanted to leave me everything. Part of me thinks it's because he had no one else, but in reality, he probably wanted to keep up pretenses even in death."

"But then you're coming back?"

"I planned on coming back here whether you liked it or not."

"Oh really?"

"Mm-hmm. I figured if you didn't let me back, your men would have your head if they had to put up with any more of your cooking." She didn't know that she wanted to cook long-term but she'd found that she really liked it.

His hands drifted to her waist. "You're right about that. So...are you staying here permanently?"

"Well, I have a Master's in social work and if there's an opportunity to work somewhere else around here, I might take the job." She didn't even want to think that far ahead though.

"You still didn't answer my question."

"What question would that be?" She pursed her lips into a thin line to keep from smiling.

"Are you going to stay here permanently? With me?" His grip tightened and he scowled at her.

"You mean permanently in Lake City?"

He rolled his eyes. "Okay, I guess I can add difficult to the list."

"What list?"

"The mental list I've been making of all your attributes. Bossy, difficult, sneaky—"

"Sneaky?"

"You did hide a few important facts about yourself. To be fair though, I guess I should add sexy, sweet—"

His words were muffled as she stood up and searched out his lips with her own. Before they got too carried away, she pulled her head back and grinned. "By the way, I love you too."

CHAPTER FOURTEEN

Two Weeks Later

"That's the last of it. I think we might need a new closet though." Emma stared at the dresses, coats and shoes barely stuffed into their closet.

"Maybe if you got rid of some of your shoes, there wouldn't be a problem." He glanced at her, then back at the closet with raised eyebrows.

"I guess you should have thought about that before you asked me to move in and put this thing on my finger." She half-swatted his shoulder and waggled her left hand in front of his face. Then she looked down at her hand and smiled. A three-carat marquis-cut engagement ring had seemed a little excessive but he hadn't been willing to budge. And hey, she wasn't going to argue too hard if he wanted to give her gorgeous jewelry.

"Do you feel like going out tonight?" His deep voice brought her back to the present.

"Ugh, no. Let's make it a movie night and stay in." She'd been moving at warp speed for the past couple of weeks.

"Okay, okay. How about I cook?" Laughing under his breath, he dropped a kiss on her forehead.

"Sounds good to me." She slipped her hand in his as they walked to the kitchen. His idea of cooking was popping a pizza in the oven. Since all she wanted to do was curl up on the couch with a glass of wine, his style of cooking would be more than fine.

She poured two glasses of wine while he started working on dinner. Taking her glass, she retreated to the living room and turned on the television. When her picture flashed across the screen, she cringed. During her high-speed packing and moving mission in Miami, the media had been relentless in scrutinizing her every move. That is until the FBI discovered a link between Mendez and Marcus Carrington, the stepson of presidential hopeful Thomas Carrington. Then all hell had broken loose and she was suddenly old news.

"Turn that crap off, honey. Haven't you had enough?" Caleb dropped down next to her on the couch and took the remote from her hand, immediately switching it to ESPN.

She rolled her eyes and took a sip of her wine. That was another thing she was getting used to, apart from sharing a closet. Sharing the remote. She figured it was a fair trade for hot sex, a man who loved her and who she loved in return.

Thank you for reading Running From the Past. I really hope you enjoyed it and that you'll consider leaving a review at one of your favorite online retailers. It's a great way to help other readers discover new books and I appreciate all reviews.

If you would like to read more, turn the page for a sneak peek of Bound to Danger, the second book in my Deadly Ops series. And if you don't want to miss any future releases, please feel free to join my newsletter. I only send out a newsletter for new releases or sales news. Find the signup link on my website: http://www.katiereus.com

BOUND TO DANGER

Deadly Ops Series
Copyright © 2014 Katie Reus

Forcing her body to obey her when all she wanted to do was curl into a ball and cry until she passed out, she got up. Cool air rushed over her exposed back and backside as her feet hit the chilly linoleum floor. She wasn't wearing any panties and the hospital gown wasn't covering much of her. She didn't care.

Right now she didn't care about much at all.

Sometime when she'd been asleep her dirty, rumpled gown had been removed from the room. And someone had left a small bag of clothes on the bench by the window. No doubt Nash had brought her something to wear. He'd been in to see her a few times, but she'd asked him to leave each time. She felt like a complete bitch because she knew he just wanted to help, but she didn't care. Nothing could help, and being alone with her pain was the only way she could cope right now.

Feeling as if she were a hundred years old, she'd started unzipping the small brown leather bag when the door opened. As she turned to look over her shoulder, she found Nash, a uniformed police officer, and another really tall, thuggish-looking man entering.

Her eyes widened in recognition. The tattoos were new, but the *thug* was Cade O'Reilly. He'd served in the Marines with her brother. They'd been best friends and her brother, Riel, named after her father, had even brought him home a few times. But that was years ago. Eight to be exact. It was hard to forget the man who'd completely cut her out of his life after her brother died, as if she meant nothing to him.

Cade towered over Nash—who was pretty tall himself—and had a sleeve of tattoos on one arm and a couple on the other. His jet-black hair was almost shaved, the skull trim close to his head, just like the last time she'd seen him. He was . . . intimidating. Always had been. And startlingly handsome in that badboy way she was sure had made plenty of women . . . Yeah, she wasn't even going there.

She swiveled quickly, putting her back to the window so she wasn't flashing them. Reaching around to her back, she clasped the hospital gown together. "You can't knock?" she practically shouted, her voice raspy from crying, not sure whom she was directing the question to.

"I told them you weren't to be bothered, but—"

The police officer cut Nash off, his gaze kind but direct. "Ms. Cervantes, this man is from the NSA and needs to ask you some questions. As soon as you're done, the doctors will release you."

"I know who he is." She bit the words out angrily, earning a surprised look from Nash and a controlled look from Cade.

She might know Cade, or she had at one time, but she hadn't known he worked for the NSA. After her brother's death he'd stopped communicating with her. Her brother had brought him home during one of their short leaves, and she and Cade had become friends. *Good friends.* They'd e-mailed all the time, for almost a year straight. Right near the end of their long correspondence, things had shifted between them, had been heading into more than friendly territory. Then after Riel died, it was as if Cade had too. It had cut her so deep to lose him on top of her brother. And now he showed up in the hospital room after her mom's death and wanted to talk to her? Hell no.

She'd been harassing the nurses to find a doctor who would discharge her, and now she knew why they'd been putting her off. They'd done a dozen tests and she didn't have a brain injury. She wasn't exhibiting any signs of having a concussion except for the memory loss, but the doctors were convinced that this was because of shock and trauma at what she'd apparently witnessed.

Nash started to argue, but the cop hauled him away, talking in low undertones, shutting the door behind them. Leaving her alone with this giant of a man.

Feeling raw and vulnerable, Maria wrapped her arms around herself. The sun had almost set, so even standing by the window didn't warm her up. She just felt so damn cold. Because of the room and probably grief. And now to be faced with a dark reminder of her past was too much.

Red Stone Security Series
No One to Trust
Danger Next Door
Fatal Deception
Miami, Mistletoe & Murder
His to Protect
Breaking Her Rules
Protecting His Witness
Sinful Seduction
Under His Protection

The Serafina: Sin City Series
First Surrender
Sensual Surrender
Sweetest Surrender
Dangerous Surrender

Deadly Ops Series
Targeted
Bound to Danger

Non-series Romantic Suspense
Running From the Past
Everything to Lose

Dangerous Deception
Dangerous Secrets
Killer Secrets
Deadly Obsession
Danger in Paradise
His Secret Past

Paranormal Romance
Destined Mate
Protector's Mate
A Jaguar's Kiss
Tempting the Jaguar
Enemy Mine
Heart of the Jaguar

Moon Shifter Series
Alpha Instinct
Lover's Instinct (novella)
Primal Possession
Mating Instinct
His Untamed Desire (novella)
Avenger's Heat
Hunter Reborn

Darkness Series
Darkness Awakened
Taste of Darkness

ABOUT THE AUTHOR

Katie Reus is the *New York Times* and *USA Today* bestselling author of the Red Stone Security series, the Moon Shifter series and the Deadly Ops series. She fell in love with romance at a young age thanks to books she pilfered from her mom's stash. Years later she loves reading romance almost as much as she loves writing it.

However, she didn't always know she wanted to be a writer. After changing majors many times, she finally graduated summa cum laude with a degree in psychology. Not long after that she discovered a new love. Writing. She now spends her days writing dark paranormal romance and sexy romantic suspense.

For more information on Katie please visit her website: www.katiereus.com. Also find her on twitter @katiereus or visit her on facebook at: www.facebook.com/katiereusauthor.

Made in the USA
San Bernardino, CA
10 July 2016